Annabella

Cloaked In Loneliness

Book One

Manhanset House
Shelter Island Hts., New York 11965-0342

bricktower@aol.com • absolutelyamazingebooks.com

Library of Congress Cataloging-in-Publication Data
Kumor, Renee.
Annabella—Cloaked In Loneliness
p. cm.

1. FICTION / Romance / Suspense. 2. FICTION / Mystery & Detective /
Hard-Boiled. 3. FICTION / Thrillers / Crime. Fiction, I. Title.
ISBN: 978-1-1955036-98-6, Trade Paper

December 2025

Annabella

Cloaked In Loneliness

Book One

Renee Kumor

Habent Sua Fata Libelli

Books in the *River Bend Chronicles'* Series by Renee Kumor

CHAPTER 1

The sounds of the train were hypnotic. Annabella Chase Winters sighed, but only inside herself. Years of self-reliance and loneliness had taught her to always present a placid, bland face to the world. No shoulder shrugging in regret or despair. No deep sighs of frustration came out of her mouth in loud breaths. No harsh stares. No sarcastic tilt of her head. No foot stomping. She swallowed another quiet, inner sigh. She had schooled herself to do nothing, act in no way that indicated emotion to anyone who might be looking at her. And that was such a farfetched notion itself because who would be looking at someone who was invisible? None the less she had schooled herself to move slowly, calmly, staying erect, a posture that defined her inner strength, and never showed her inner despair, or inner lack of life, lack of hope, lack of everything except an overwhelming demand, by her body, but not her soul, to breathe in and breathe out.

She was on her way to another change in her life, a change that was not her first choice, but her last option. Ten years ago, three weeks after her nineteenth birthday, her parents died. For a year she and her brother shared the house and shared a life. She finished her training at the teachers' ordinary and became certified as an instructor. At the same time her brother made plans to marry. One day he approached her to talk about the future. "Annabella," he began in a voice that he was using now that he was head teller at the bank, "I think that you should move on. I want to bring my wife into this house, and you might find it an uncomfortable situation." He had gripped his lapels, much the way she was certain he did at the bank, as he continued, "You have your certificate and I'll give you the cash for your share of this house and property. I'll be mighty fair because I know my responsibilities to you. I've done some research and I know you can find a teaching position anywhere in this country."

"Anywhere in the country?" she had gasped. Those were the days when she showed emotion. "You want me to leave Cincinnati? And where am I to go?"

"Now, I didn't say that you should leave Cincinnati," he had backpedaled, "I just mean you have the world at your feet. Why, you can travel. See the country. Find some fellow." Because they both knew that no Cincinnati fellow was in the picture. She was well into her twentieth year of age with no prospects so far. "I have a banking friend in St. Louis who thinks he can be of help. He's waiting for your letter of inquiry. He'll help you find something."

The wedding was planned for September and Annabella knew that her brother wanted her gone before then. He didn't seem to care whether she attended his wedding or not. Annabella talked with her friends and corresponded with the man in St. Louis. Her friends, there were only two, encouraged her to go for the adventure. They told her she could be independent and support herself with a teaching opportunity. She would probably find a rich fellow in St. Louis. Of course, both of her friends would be married before the summer was over. Which meant that by September she would be the only unmarried person in her small circle of friends and relatives.

xxx

It was a boring and dusty train ride from southeast Colorado to the northern Wyoming territory. But Will Rutherford, a young, prosperous rancher, always enjoyed watching people on trains during his travels. He was returning to the family ranch after purchasing some livestock and meeting with some bankers on the family's behalf. He had sent the livestock ahead with the drovers and was enjoying a leisurely return by train, happy to forego several nights under a trail blanket eating cold beans.

He slumped in the corner of the last seat of the passenger car with his hat low over his shrewd, gray eyes. Years of travel had taught him to adopt this pose, the best way to discourage traveling salesmen and preachers from getting friendly. He had heard enough yarns to last his lifetime. Right now he was watching that woman several seats ahead. She was wearing a prim travel outfit in a dark green plaid. She wasn't beautiful, although she had a rich looking head of dark brown hair peeking out from under her travel bonnet. She was interesting, however, because she didn't move. She sat like a statue, never glancing to watch other passengers, never moving to stretch her legs during the several stops, never speaking to any of the other women who were also traveling on the train.

Will had walked through the train car at the previous stop and walked back just to see her face. She might as well have been wax like those displays he had heard about in the big cities. She never looked at him as he passed but continued to stare out the window. He found her intriguing as something to study on the trip home.

Home! He and his brother Dell owned the ranch, the Rocking R. Dell was the brains and, as their mother used to say, Will was the charm. Dell stayed on the ranch and kept it prosperous. Will worked the road, buying and selling and making future contacts. Both men were happy with their assigned roles. Sometimes Will worried about Dell. It wasn't natural for a man to keep so much to himself. Not like Will who had enjoyed several ladies during this trip. Of course, he kept that side of him quiet back home. He was sort of courting. He had been giving a lot of thought to the preacher's daughter. She was a tiny little thing with a beautiful singing voice and a sparkle in her blue eyes. She just wasn't quite ready yet to be a rancher's wife. He thought the little lady needed a year or two to mature because life on the ranch would be harsh and lonely. He had been talking to her about that life, but she didn't seem to hear what he was saying.

In fact, during this trip he had almost decided to pull back his interest for the time being. Since Dell wasn't looking at any women, the two brothers could just carry on as they had for a bit longer. They would probably just grow old together, grizzly bachelors like Henry Winters and his two ranch hands.

That thought made Will's stomach sink. He didn't want to be a grizzled bachelor, he wanted a wife and family. He took a deep breath and settled in his seat as the train rattled along, the lady statue still not moving.

xxx

Annabella was lost in her usual daydreams as the train moved closer to her new life. She smirked inwardly. No life was a better description of her situation than 'new life.' She would continue to breathe, to eat and to sleep - that's what she did now - but she never considered any of it a life.

She thought back to her first move - to St. Louis. She had made inquiries of her brother's friend, the banker. He promised to help her find a position. He had made no other promises and Annabella, foolishly, read more than existed into the letters. With the promise of a job, and maybe romance, she had accepted the cash from her brother, which he thoughtfully transferred to St. Louis so she wouldn't lose the money or be robbed on her trip.

In St. Louis she learned some lessons, not hard, mean lessons, but hurtful, discouraging lessons on how invisible she was. The banker had proved to be just as his letters stated, a man who helped her find a teaching position. He had a wife and family and a busy social life that didn't include women who worked for a living at such menial tasks as teaching his children.

Sitting alone in her room provided by the school and working with several other young women at a modest, but respectable institution, became her life. Many of her colleagues lived within a short distance of family. They had personal lives to see to after hours. She had nothing but her books and her room.

In her first year she became acquainted with other boarders and fashioned a minor social life at dinner and joined a church for some social activity on weekends. No St. Louis fellow appeared in her life and the teachers at her school seemed to work for a year or two and then marry and move on to another kind of life and move permanently out of her life.

These were the years Annabella began to master her emotions and control of the face that only her students ever seemed to see. Why, she had wondered, should she smile at dinner when no one looked at her? Why should she worry over another's tragedy when no one thought she could be of help? Why shrug as an answer to a question when no one ever asked? By the third year in St. Louis, she had learned that she was expected to teach her students and not intrude in the lives of anyone outside of her classroom.

As she completed her third year, she had been at the school longer than anyone save the headmaster. He had seemed to be challenged by her talent and intelligence. One day he said, "Miss Chase, I have received a request from a school in Wichita looking for a teacher of experience to become a member of a faculty and take some leadership responsibilities."

Annabella's heart sort of fluttered. A strange feeling because in three years nothing had happened in her life to encourage any thrill. "Yes, sir. Thank you for bringing this to my attention. Do you think I could do the job as it has been described to you?"

"You certainly can," he huffed and puffed as he usually did when he wanted to be perceived as all-knowing. "I have suggested that you are what they need. They are looking forward to your inquiry."

Annabella was startled out of her daydream as the train seemed to swerve. She looked around her. Had she fallen asleep? Had the conductor called? She listened, looked around and was surprised to find a small girl sitting on the seat beside her. Annabella smiled a rare soft smile at the youngster. The little girl gave a shy smile in return.

xxx

Will was suddenly alert. He had noticed that several children were in another car disembarking in clusters at each station. They must be orphans, he thought - kids being sent to ranchers and other folks along the way who were willing to take in a healthy youngster in exchange for work. He didn't know what he thought about that arrangement. He supposed some folks were good to the kids and some folks were not.

He and Dell were orphans. Over the last five years they had lost both parents. Of course, they were grown men at the time and already running the ranch. But still there was no mama to cook and no pappy to offer advice. He did miss them, but they had been good folks and taught their sons well. Their passing left something Will thought of as a warm sadness. He had had them once and could always remember, but he sometimes missed them mightily.

He continued to watch the train car activity. The orphans were getting restless. He saw a youngster mosey into the car and quietly pass what looked like a piece of bread to the shelf above the seats. A small hand reached out from above, then the blanket and carpet bag resettled as though nothing was amiss. Later a little girl with curly strawberry hair quietly walked through the train and then back toward his seat. She studied the passengers then chose to sit beside the statue lady.

Will pushed his hat back so he could see better. The lady looked at the little girl. The girl gave her a shy nod. Then the youngster smiled at another little girl and moved to chat with her. The statue lady returned to her frozen position.

xxx

As the little girl moved on, Annabella continued her reverie. She recalled leaving St. Louis. She had taken the suggestion of the headmaster and applied for the job in Wichita. Three more years of lonely living had followed. She was appreciated as a qualified educator, but she was getting old and spinsterly. School board members liked hiring fresh young things. And the single men in the community favored the younger recruits for wifely potential. When Annabella arrived in Wichita she was written off as old, but competent, and ignored.

As she was completing her third year at the Wichita school, Annabella overheard a discussion between two school board members. She was cleaning her classroom and a window was open. The term would be ending, and she was preparing for another lonely summer where she would find extra work at odd jobs doing correspondence for elderly ladies, taking in sewing for other boarders and work two days a week for a local doctor keeping his records and other paperwork organized. In fact, these small jobs kept her busy all through the school year and filled her evenings and weekends. She always put the extra money into her account. Having no social life helped her savings grow.

Under the window of her classroom the men were speaking. One had said, "We have to pay her more money. She's been here three years."

The other had said, "Or we just don't renew her contract and hire one of those pretty young teachers that has applied."

"You know, she's not bad to look at," offered the first man. "A little skinny. If she only smiled." There had been silence. Then, "Where would she go? She does have students and parents here who value her skill."

"Leave it to me."

Within the week Annabella had been approached by a member of the school board. "Miss Chase," he began, "I have received an inquiry from a friend in Pueblo, Colorado. They are developing a fine school system and are looking for teachers with experience to help them staff their upper school.

Annabella had been expecting something and this was it. She knew that she had been encouraged to leave St. Louis but was not certain why. She was being encouraged to leave Wichita, and she knew why. There was no role for an experienced, talented, female as an administrator or supervisor in public schools. Six lonely years had schooled her in the realities. "Thank you for thinking I'm qualified for this opportunity." She nodded to the gentleman, never showing her thoughts, hurts and disappointments.

"Fine, fine. They'll be interested in your inquiry."

She had wondered if she should even inform her brother of this latest displacement. In six years, he had never replied to any correspondence. She sighed, as she had taught herself, with no visible outer sign, when she thought about Pueblo and another change.

She informed all of her students and all of her clients that she would be leaving. No one had seemed concerned. She offered names of other teachers who would step in to write letters and work for the doctor.

Within a week she had been certain no one in Wichita would notice any inconvenience - or even remember her.

After two years in Pueblo Annabella had been ready to take the initiative and move on. She was surprised at this decision, but her living circumstances were beyond lonely. Some days she had been surprised she was still breathing. She taught acceptable students, but never saw that she made an impression, that they would recognize her on the street. She searched for a friendly church and never found a welcoming congregation.

One day as she paged through a newspaper, she had noticed an ad for a wife. In a small, nearby town a man, widowed with a son, was advertising for a woman to take on the responsibilities of wife, mother and unpaid helper in the family business.

She had replied to the ad. To her surprise, she received a telegram from the gentleman saying he would be in Pueblo on business and would like to meet. They met. He affirmed his offer; she accepted. She finished out the remaining weeks of her contract. The man, Mr. Winters, had returned to Pueblo, stood with her before a judge and escorted her to Fort Collins where he managed a mercantile. They would live above the store. The boy was eleven.

As the train rattled and swayed, Annabella thought about her marriage, such as it was. She and Mr. Winters came to an agreement regarding marriage rights. They held the discussion as they traveled back to Fort Collins on the train after they had exchanged vows.

"Ma'am," he had said after clearing his throat several times. "I'd appreciate if you would consider consenting to wifely duties." The train had shimmied over the track bed.

Annabella remembered that she had thought about his request for what must have been several miles. Finally, she said, "Mr. Winters, I agree that I owe you some respect for honoring me with your protection. I believe your request is reasonable. But you must understand that I have no experience."

From the corner of her eye, she had seen him flex his hands. "Ma'am, I understand. I will be respectful of your sensibilities."

And that had been how she became a wife. Every Saturday night, after a bath, Mr. Winters had reached for her in their bed and slowly initiated her to wifely duties. He was a kind and gentle man. He was respectful and appreciative. He liked the way she treated his son. He liked her cooking. He praised her cleanliness and organization. And finally, after two or three months he had asked, "Ma'am, do you think you could kiss me a time or two and embrace me?"

"Certainly, Mr. Winters. Please instruct me in the ways you want me to respond."

He did and she learned to caress, to rub his shoulders, to kiss his mouth and to sometimes even kiss his ear. There were even times when she thought she felt a thrill. But the feeling passed so quickly. For his kindness and protection, though, she had tried to give him warmth and comfort - every Saturday night.

Then one day she was a widow after less than a year of marriage. Mr. Winters and his son were killed in an accident when their wagon overturned as they returned from making a delivery to an outlying ranch. The owner of the mercantile had said he could not allow a lone woman to operate the store. He had permitted her to stay in the living quarters until she made other arrangements and to assist the new manager, as he phrased it, "in return for housing."

During this transition time her life took an interesting turn and Annabella saw it as a sign - whether good or bad, she wasn't sure. At Mr. Winters' death, she wrote a letter to his father who ranched in Wyoming Territory. The Winters family had planned to visit the ranch when the school year concluded. The deaths ended that plan. But the elder Mr. Winters wrote to Annabella:

Dear Daughter,
You are my only kin. Come to Wyoming. Make your life with me. I know you cared for my son and grandson in an honorable manner. My son wrote of your many good qualities. You are welcome here.

Your father,
Henry Winters

It had taken her two weeks to reply to Mr. Winters, accept his invitation, clean the living quarters, and then plan her way to his ranch. Fortunately, the train made a stop at the small town closest to the ranch. Mr. Winters had told her he would come to town a day or two after the train was scheduled to arrive. She was to stay at the home of the Presbyterian minister and his wife. Women were not welcome, unaccompanied, in hotels.

The conductor announced the next stop bringing her out of her reverie. He glanced at Annabella. "This is your station, ma'am, Deep Wells."

xxx

When the conductor announced that they were arriving, Will watched as the statue-like lady pulled her gloves over her hands, gathered her book and bag while the little girl who seemed to be watching her moved to a seat just behind her. The train stopped. Will always waited to be the last off, not interested in the crowding, and he watched as the lady moved forward, the little girl trailing close behind - never touching or talking but moving as though she was a shadow.

The rancher thought that action was very interesting, but even more interesting was the young fellow who passed through the car as it emptied. He dragged down the bag from the upper shelf and helped a small boy out of the bag. He pushed the little guy toward the exit emptying onto the platform as the older boy followed, his eyes watching for any unwelcome activity coming from behind. It was an interesting parade - the statue lady, the strawberry haired girl, the little fellow and the older boy.

Those children made Will curious. Something was up. He wondered if they were working together, or if they were orphans separated from the others. The little girl and the little boy didn't look like candidates for some farmer to claim as potential workers. In fact, the little boy didn't look like he even could speak much. What were they up to?

CHAPTER 2

Annabella nodded a 'thank you' to the conductor as he took her travel bag and helped her from the train. As she stepped from the train he said, "I'll have your trunks unloaded to the platform. You can send for them when you're settled." She nodded. She glanced at the other passengers pushing onto the congested platform as she held tightly to her small parcels moving away from the frenzy. She glanced at the activity - arriving and departing travelers, trunks lifted onto carriages, people hugging hello and farewell - the usual platform activities. Wanting to avoid the confusion of those disembarking and boarding the train, Annabella moved along the platform, finding a quiet shaded spot beside the depot. Sometimes she felt invisible in a crowd. Who looked at a spinster? Who noticed if she smiled or frowned? But she was here now -beginning a new life? Could that be possible – to begin to live - after so many years of just breathing? She watched the comings and goings, wondering if the preacher would find an invisible woman.

There seemed to be a lot of children tumbling out from one of the other train cars. They shouted and pushed and shoved as restless children would. She silently watched as a man tried to organize them, shouting, cursing, slapping. The man turned to the local folks and announced, "I got these orphans. They's willing to work. They need homes. Some of you have made claims. Any others interested see me. We got thirty minutes before we leave for the next stop." Several people held yellow flyers and looked as though they had come to the train to select one of the youngsters.

Annabella watched as folks looked over the children. She wondered if this was how the slave markets had operated decades ago. But there didn't seem to be money involved here at the depot, nor an auction. In this case, someone with a need for a young healthy boy could promise to feed and shelter one in exchange for work. No one would challenge the promise, and no one would make certain the exchange was fair.

Almost like her new situation, thought Annabella. She had no idea what circumstances she would find with Mr. Winters. What would be asked of her in return for food and shelter? Her mind drifted again as she tried to imagine the future and she was startled back to the present when the orphans' man came to her. "You claiming these youngsters?"

"What?" She felt a pull on her skirt and looked down at the little girl from the train. "Where did you come from?"

Behind her a young boy's voice whispered, "She's ours."

Annabella glanced around. She seemed to be surrounded by children. Before she could speak, a tall, handsome man walked up beside her, grinned and said, "We need a few hands to help with the farm. We'll take good care of them."

The orphan man surveyed the little group, moved his lips silently as he counted. "You need six?" He was amazed. No one ever took more than two.

Annabella opened her mouth in shock, but the tall man spoke again. "We got a big ranch." His grin was innocent and open as he threw his arms around two of the boys.

"Now look here," began the orphan man, "I got to make certain things are decent . . ."

"Things will be decent," said a man on horseback. No one had noticed his arrival. He had a rugged look and resembled the stranger at Annabella's side. "We hired this lady to help us take care of the smaller youngsters." He nodded to the orphan man who seemed to sputter and gave a very businesslike nod to Annabella.

"I just have to be certain." The orphan man scratched his chin.

"You can," replied the man on horseback. "You ask folks around here. We're the Rutherford brothers. We got a mighty fine cattle spread."

"I heard of you," said the orphan man, in awe. "You're known in these parts." He quickly scanned the children. The little girl still held on to Annabella's skirt with one hand but seemed to be holding onto a smaller boy with the other. The man smashed his hat more securely on his head, muttered, "Six young'uns," and walked away shouting to all the unclaimed children, "Get back on that train."

The whistle blew, the conductor shouted and soon the train was leaving the station. Within minutes, the bustle of the platform area had subsided. Annabella stood with the children as though watching a staged drama. What had happened? "Ma'am," said the man on horseback, tipping his hat. "That was mighty reckless, claiming all these youngsters. What will you do with them?"

She gaped at the man. After almost ten years of numbing boredom and loneliness, suddenly she was catapulted into living - talking with confusing strangers and possessing six children. Before she could respond, one of the older boys said, "He's not ours." And pointed to the small boy holding the little girl's hand.

"He's mine." The dark-eyed boy of about ten stepped out from behind Annabella. "They took his shoes. We had to get away." The little boy who appeared to be not much older than three or maybe four stood barefooted in the dirt.

Annabella studied the children. Four of them were clearly related, each fair-skinned and freckled, topped with heads of red hair from strawberry to flame. The other two boys were dark haired and dark-eyed. All of them were thin and dirty.

The man on horseback looked back at a red-haired boy who seemed the oldest, maybe sixteen or so. "What's your story?"

"Us four are together. I'm Will, this is Toby," a boy of about fourteen, "Molly," he pointed to a girl of about twelve, "and Missy." He nodded toward the little girl who was maybe eight. "Me and Toby didn't like the way some of those older boys looked at Molly."

"My name's Will, too," said the brother of the small boy, "and he's Byron."

"Mighty big name for such a little fellow," said the tall man standing next to Annabella. And I'm Will, too." He wiggled his eyebrows at the children and the girls giggled. "And that's my brother Dell." He nodded to the man on horseback.

They all looked at the woman standing with them. She looked at each youngster and finally spoke to the man on horseback, "I'm Annabella Winters. I've come to visit my father-in-law."

"I heard his son died," said Dell.

"Yes, I'm his widow. Mr. Winters invited me to stay since I'm his only relative now that my husband is dead." Annabella spoke as she always spoke, clearly and with little emotion. "I am to be met by a minister and am to lodge with his family until Mr. Winters gets to town."

"Excuse me," interrupted a chubby, bald man, "Did I hear you say you're Mrs. Winters?" He looked at the gang of children. "My, my, we can't house all of you. I had no idea."

Annabella opened her mouth to speak, but Will Rutherford said, "That's fine, Reverend, we'll get them out to the Winters' place." He kept his eyes on the children because he didn't want to see the shock, and probably a little anger, in Dell's eyes.

The reverend, happy to be relieved of the burden said, "Mighty fine idea. Thank you fellows for being so accommodating." He nodded to Annabella and Dell, then said, "Now, Will, you don't be a stranger, Margaret Ann looks forward to your visits."

The grin slid from Will's face, but he nodded and turned his attention to his brother, because between Margaret Ann and Dell, he would choose Dell. The reverend bustled off to pray or something and Will said to his brother, "You musta brought a wagon to get some supplies. We can take these folks to old man Winters. I don't have much gear."

Dell climbed down from his horse and handed the lines to one of the boys. He walked over to Annabella. "Ma'am, we'll see that you all get to the Winters' place. But I think you should bring some extra food and maybe some clothes for these youngsters. This little fellow needs shoes." He looked more closely at the other children then back at Annabella. "Do you have funds?"

Annabella had been caught up by life before, pulled along without the ability to take a stand, unable to speak for her own preferences, or to stop the slow momentum of life dragging her along. She silently stared at Dell. He didn't pressure her to reply because he seemed to understand that she was processing the situation and organizing her response. He seemed to be giving her a chance to walk away or to dive in - it was her decision to make. Her sense told her that these two men, these brothers, would step in and care for the children if she walked away. That gave her pause. Were there really folks in the world who would step in, who could see the hunger, loneliness, fear, in others? Which sort of person would she be now that life gave her the opportunity to step?

She cleared her throat and asked, "Mr. Rutherford, can you tell me what would happen to these children if I leave them here?"

He thought for a moment. "As you heard, my harebrained brother seems to have committed us to their protection. However, our ranch doesn't have any women and I would worry about the girls and the little fellow." He tilted his head to Missy and Byron. "We could take the older boys, but they would have to work and might not see their kin for weeks."

Annabella processed his response. "What are the conditions at Mr. Winters' ranch?"

"He has a squaw who cooks for him and two ranch hands. He also has a much smaller spread. The youngsters would all stay together, probably help with the chores. He might enjoy the company."

"Is he a good man?" Collecting information, processing responses, nothing more was reflected in her demeanor.

"He's a fair man. He takes care of his ranch workers and he doesn't drink or play cards." Dell didn't want to say anything about loose women or sex because everyone on the plateau knew that old man Winters had been bedding his squaw for many years.

"I have funds," she said as she thought about all the years she had saved because she had no reason, no life, to use those funds. "I can furnish supplies and clothing for the children. I am a trained teacher," the boys moaned, "and I am well organized. What would be appropriate to bring with us to the ranch?" Her decision was made. She was a trained teacher. What would be different than her work with her students?

Dell said, "We can go to the mercantile. My wagon is there. You should buy some flour and other basics. They have a good vegetable garden at the ranch and meat, of course. The youngsters will need boots and work pants and shirts. I'd get the girls," he scanned her up and down, "and you, trousers also. Sometimes a woman is safer on the range if she doesn't look like a woman."

Safer? Annabella maintained her façade of reserve as she absorbed the implications of Mr. Rutherford's observations. "Thank you for that advice, Mr. Rutherford." She glanced over her shoulder. "I have a trunk on the platform and a few boxes. The children may have things." They all shook their heads. She felt a strange sadness - no belongings?

Dell gave one wordless look to his brother and Will ordered, "Give Dell back his horse and you big guys follow me." He was off with the three older boys. Dell lifted Byron and Missy and placed them on his horse, instructing Missy to hold on to Byron. He started leading the horse to the mercantile. Annabella handed Molly her parcels, picked up the remaining bag and walked at his side while Missy and Byron grinned with pleasure at the turn of events.

"Ma'am, if Winters has a problem, my brother and I will try to help . . ." He didn't know what they could do, accommodating six children would be a challenge.

"Thank you, Mr. Rutherford. I've managed a classroom for eight years and ran a household for one." She looked at him, no smile, no challenge, just a pleasant distant air about her.

"Excuse me, ma'am," asked Dell, "You were only married for one year?"

"Yes," she replied in her calm, but distant manner, "I answered an ad. Mr. Winters had lost his wife and was left to raise his son alone. We married about a year ago and managed quite well, until his death."

Dell had nothing more to say and neither did Annabella. They walked in silence as the two smaller children giggled and Molly skipped along in a lighthearted manner, all three children reflecting an optimism that they had not enjoyed just an hour before.

At the mercantile Will already had all Annabella's belongings in the wagon. An older man sat on the driver's bench as the boys scrambled to the rancher's orders. Annabella said, "Mr. Rutherford, I'll deal with the girls first if you could please assist me. I'm certain your brother can entertain the boys." Dell helped the children from the horse. Annabella took Byron from his arms and carried him into the shop. The girls and Dell followed.

Within thirty minutes the children were sitting in the wagon, Byron admiring his new shoes, and the girls clutching packages. The man from the mercantile loaded the other purchases as Annabella instructed the children. "Girls, you will sit in the wagon and Byron, you stay with the girls and enjoy your shoes while I shop with the boys. And here." She handed out small hard candies to each of the youngsters in the wagon. The older boys seemed to object. She turned to them. "They behaved in the shop, listened to instructions, and helped one another. They deserve a reward." She raised an eyebrow and looked at the older boys.

"Yes, ma'am," came three meek replies.

Dell and Will exchanged glances. Maybe there was more to Annabella than there appeared at first glance.

Finally all the children and all the purchases were in the wagon. Before she climbed aboard, Annabella signaled to Dell. "How long is the ride to the ranch? And what can we feed these children?"

Dell lifted his hat from his head and resettled it more securely. "Ma'am, we should get to the ranch a little after dark. It's seven or eight miles, but a long pull up a grade. I can stop at the restaurant," he nodded toward a small shop with a sign that said 'Eats' "and have them pack us up some food."

She reached into her pocket and pulled a small sack, "I can give you some money."

"Ma'am, me and Will and my driver'll eat more than you and those youngsters. We'll buy the food. There's a nice spot just outside of town by the river." She nodded and he walked away.

"Oh, Mr. Rutherford," she called, "please bring some towels so the children can wash up before they eat." The boys moaned again.

The wagon left town as Dell stopped at the diner. Soon he was coming up behind them with a basket tied to the back of his horse.

The picnic spot was all that Dell promised, fresh grass, a small, cool stream to wash and to play in. Annabella took responsibility for cleaning the children while the men, especially the driver, a pleasant fellow named Grandy, set out the food and arranged some blankets and rocks for seating. After a fine meal, the children asked for time to play in the water - even the older boys enjoyed the free time. Grandy volunteered to watch the children while the other adults finished the meal and cleaned up.

As the men ate Will turned to Dell. "The talk about statehood is heating up. They expect a vote here and in the US Senate soon."

"I told you before," growled Dell, "those politicians can just leave us alone. We're doing fine."

"But they've been talking about water rights."

Dell scowled again. "I think they settled water rights on our land when they assigned the land."

Annabella looked confused. "You have no water?"

Dell shook his head. "No, all this talk about statehood and those fools included water and irrigation in the discussion. When our folks got their land, the government made certain everyone on the plateau had access to water. He thought a moment. "Pretty good idea. None of us fights the other for water." He dug into his meal.

"They were thinking about you, too, ma'am," offered Will. "Some of those politicians want to give women the right to vote. So statehood will make you a voter."

Annabella gave him a long thoughtful look. "I seem to have the same regard for politicians as your brother does."

Will barked out a laugh. Dell gave her a small smile and changed the subject. With a glance at the children, he asked, "What do you think their stories are?" He nodded toward the four siblings with variations of red hair. The girls' hair glowing a soft red blond and the two boys with aggressive red, untamed hair.

"I'm certain we'll learn their story in time," replied Annabella. She watched the other two boys who stayed close together. The older brother was protective toward his younger sibling. All of the children looked as though they had missed several meals and were growing out of their clothing. She found each one as endearing as the next and marveled at the care and responsibility the older siblings had for the younger. Too bad her brother never considered his responsibility to his sister. But Annabella chided herself with a warning not to feel sorry for herself. Life has just handed you a purpose, she told herself, and maybe an adventure. She began to wonder what Mr. Winters would do with her and her orphans. Was there a future? Would she find a life, an adventure? Was this real or one of her daydreams? Though these thoughts worked through her mind, as usual, no ideas or feelings reflected in her face.

CHAPTER 3

"You got too many Wills," said Will Rutherford.

"I don't understand," replied Annabella, pulling herself mentally back to the picnic site. Daydreaming was becoming a luxury that she would have to abandon with so many children to oversee.

"Two of those boys are named Will." Then he grinned. "And you got me."

A smile, an unusual phenomenon, skittered across her face. "But the boys won't be living with you." He frowned. "Oh," gasped Annabella, "I think I understand." She asked, "Have you a suggestion?"

"I say, since I'm the oldest I get to be Will and the two boys pick other names." He lowered his voice. "Then no one in your household gets to keep the name while another gives it up."

Annabella studied the young rancher. "Very astute, Mr. Rutherford. We should propose it to the boys."

He whistled and all the children came at once. They fell to the grass and gave all their attention to Annabella. A fact that Dell found interesting. The children were ready to listen to her. She began by saying, "-Children, we are starting on a great adventure. We will meet Mr. Winters and see if he will accept us as part of his family."

"We'll be a family?" asked Molly in awe.

19

"All of us?" asked the Will who was Byron's brother.

"All of us," Annabella assured them. "If we cannot stay with Mr. - Winters, Mr. Rutherford has offered to help us find a home where we can be a family. But we have a small problem." Their faces dissolved into frowns. Missy climbed into her older brother's lap and started to cry.

Will Rutherford interrupted. "It's no big problem. It's my problem. I'm Will and we have two other Wills. But I'm the oldest. So I've been Will the longest." He looked at the offending Wills. "What should we do about all the Wills?"

Will, Molly's older brother said, "I'd like to be called Patrick. That was our daddy's name, but he got killed in a mine." His sister Molly took his hand and smiled her approval.

Will, Byron's brother, cleared his throat. "I might like to be called Skeeter. That's what my pop called me when I was a young'un."

The remaining Will said, "By golly, you all solved Miss Annabella's problem. That's sure how a family works." All the kids smiled.

Dell noticed that little Byron had climbed into Grandy's lap and was falling asleep. "I think it's time we settle into the wagon." He folded the picnic blankets and created a small area where Missy and Byron could sleep as all the others claimed their seats and talked about the new adventure.

Dell allowed the wagon to pull ahead as he saddled his horse. Within a few minutes he was trailing behind the crowded wagon and was startled to see a change. Each of the children sitting up wore a broad brimmed hat. And Annabella wore one also. It looked like a wagon filled with sleepy cowboys. He again marveled that Annabella was not what she seemed and not what a man expected from a widow and a schoolteacher. Too bad she was so reserved - graceful, poised, but no laughter. Old man Winters would see to that. Dell grinned. That man was a character, and he would enjoy this mismatched family.

They reached the grade in an hour. Taking a break, Dell assessed strength and walking shoes. He and Will repacked the wagon, then he assigned seats. "Byron, you and Missy sit in the wagon and make sure nothing falls out." The serious little boy nodded. "Ma'am, you sit up with Grandy to keep the weight easy for the horses."

"I can walk, Mr. Rutherford."

"I'm sure you can, ma'am, but you need to watch those two young-sters," he explained. "Skeeter and Molly are going to ride my horse. Will and the two older boys will scout ahead to make certain nothing is blocking the trail."

"Like Indians?" asked Skeeter. His face showed that this adventure was getting better and better. Dell marveled that the new name seemed to fit the lively youngster.

"No, like big branches or boulders or washed-out places."

Will and the two older boys started the climb. Grandy got the wagon going and the four horses shuffled and pulled over rocks and twigs. Dell walked behind leading his horse with the two children astride.

It took the group about an hour to reach the top of the grade. From the ridge Annabella looked back and spied the town and the river that danced through the valley. They were now entering a forest and it was much cooler. Dell called a break at a fast-moving stream for everyone to take a drink and give the horses a rest. He surprised everyone with some bread and butter for their evening meal and Annabella had more hard candy to share with everyone.

The boys who had walked the trail took their shoes off to cool their feet in the stream. Molly complained about her bottom needing to be cooled from riding on that hard saddle. Annabella suggested that she rest her bottom on the forest floor.

"Is this your ranch land, Mr. Rutherford?" she asked. Reasonable questions in an even, polite voice.

"Ma'am, I don't mind if you call me Dell." He looked around the for-est. "On the other side of these trees is where my land begins. This here is government land. There's an old fort about ten miles that way. He pointed to his left. "Our ranch begins when we come to the fencing. And Mr. Winters's place backs up to that next ridge." He pointed to the peaks on the horizon.

"We'll be neighbors, then?" He nodded. "Please call me Annabella." She gave him a rare, soft smile as she, for one of the few times in her life, asked another person to address her by her given name.

"Dell," shouted Will. "You going to ride ahead and tell Mr. Winters we're coming?"

Dell nodded. "Good idea. I'll go when we're a little closer. I don't want to be gone and you have some wheel problems or something." Grandy and Will nodded. "Everybody back in the wagon. We're almost home."

The youngsters yawned a cheer, they were very tired.

xxx

"Hey, old man," Dell shouted as he drew close to the Winters' ranch house. The old man, his squaw and two old ranch hands tumbled out of the cabin. "I'm bringing you visitors. I met Mrs. Winters at the depot and gave her a ride."

"Now, Dell," sputtered the old man, "I was going to get her in a few days."

"Things aren't what you thought," offered Dell. "She's bringing company. Six youngsters." The old man sputtered more. The squaw studied Dell with her solemn eyes and seemed to smile at the thought of a half dozen children. Dell told them all the story of the children sneaking away from the train car full of orphans.

"She didn't turn her back on them?" asked Mr. Winters.

"Didn't bat an eye. She told me she was a wife and a teacher and could handle things."

"She ain't snooty with all her learning, is she?"

"No, sir, I think she's a fine, quiet, able woman."

"My boy liked her. He wrote me a letter and said she worked hard, took good care of him and my grandson. But he said she guarded her heart." The old man scratched his beard. "My boy was a dreamer with that flowery thinking. That's why he never took to ranching."

Dell shrugged at that description of Annabella. "I don't know about that, old man. She took charge of the youngsters and they listened. No fuss and no crying."

Henry Winters asked. "Tell me again, how many children?"

"Six."

"God almighty," moaned the old man. "We gonna be over run." He slapped his thigh and chuckled.

Once Dell had warned the Winters' ranch folks about their visitors, he rode back through the night to find the wagon. They were easy to find because the children were jabbering about the stars. It was a fresh, crisp, clear night with millions of stars littering the sky. Will was pointing out constellations and Annabella was relating the myths behind the names. Grandy was even jumping in with his own stories about how the Indians assigned stories and myths to the stars. Dell smiled to himself that Winters' ranch was never going to be the same. Then he wondered why Annabella guarded her heart.

xxx

It was almost an hour before the wagon arrived at the ranch house. By that time Mr. Winters was itching to meet his guests. They found him pacing near his smokehouse, a good lookout point on the property. He jumped into the wagon and rode up to the house trying to get to know everyone at once.

Six tired children stumbled into the small cabin. In fact, Will had to carry Byron and Dell carried Missy. Annabella steered the others into the crowded welcoming room. Mr. Winters made certain he got a good look at each person, working hard to remember names. The two ranch hands and the squaw stood at the edges of the room.

"By golly, Annabella," Mr. Winters said, "you are quite a surprise. But my son told me you were a fine lady."

Annabella was shocked at the greeting. Her husband had written about her to his father. She wondered if anyone of her acquaintance had ever referenced her in a letter before. But she had taught herself long ago to keep expression from her face, she gave the old man a nod and tilted her lips up in sort of a smile. She looked around the room as Mr. Winters said, "These are my cowpokes and my squaw." Annabella nodded. Two older men, one a Negro and one a Mexican, stood before her and nodded. Annabella held out her hand and introduced herself to each man. They smiled shyly and went off to help unload the wagon. Annabella had never shaken hands with a Negro. He shared a gentle grip with his calloused hands. This adventure would be interesting.

As her eyes met those of the squaw she shivered because she was looking into her own eyes, eyes that hid a smothering loneliness behind a face of placid repose. She walked toward the woman and held out her hand. "I'm Annabella. May I call you by name?"

Slowly the squaw reached for Annabella's hand. "I am called Morning Flower."

"What a lovely name," and a rare, sincere smile glittered on Annabella's face. "Are you responsible for the delightful aromas filling this house?"

Morning Flower nodded and grinned. "I feed you now."

"We'll help." She turned to Molly, "Let's give Morning Flower some help putting out the food." Molly seemed surprised to be included and immediately rushed to be with the women.

"I can help, too," said Missy as she wiggled out of Dell's arms.

Morning Flower assigned tasks to each of them and soon the women had quietly organized the evening snack and were herding the men toward the table. It became obvious that only half of the group could be fed at the table at one time. It was too small.

Mr. Winters surveyed the crowd in his home and said, "Tomorrow we build a bigger table."

While the children ate under the supervision of Will and Morning Flower, Annabella approached her host. "Mr. Winters, do you have space for all of us to stay with you?"

He took her hand. "Now you gotta call me Henry. 'Cause we're kin."

"All right, Henry." She pulled her hand away but patted his sleeve as a sign that she was pleased to be with him, but was unsure of their relationship, as she waited to learn about living arrangements.

Henry rubbed his grizzled chin. Then he turned to Dell. "You boys staying the night?"

"Can you accommodate us?"

"Charlie and Manuel can make space in the bunkhouse." He seemed to be mentally organizing his house and added, "The squaw and me use the room in the back. I still keep my son's room." He gave a sheepish smile to Annabella. "We were getting it ready for your visit." She nodded. Before his death she and her husband had planned to visit Henry. The old man sniffed as if caught in a memory. "We made a new bed and cleaned things. Annabella, you and those little girls can sleep in there. Them boys can sleep here in front of the stove." He nodded his head several times. "Tomorrow we build some bunks."

Annabella was startled when Henry mentioned the stove. She had seen the fireplace. Then she realized that the fireplace was on the wall in the gathering room and a wood stove for cooking was in the area designated as the kitchen. Very up to date, she thought.

Dell saw her eyeing the fireplace and spoke up. "Out here we only use the fireplace for heat in the winter. Summertime, if the nights get cold, we burn less fuel using our stoves." Annabella nodded. It was her experience that everyone learned how to survive under the conditions they found themselves. She took heart at how practical, and generous people could be. Even people who were no relation. She thought again that it had been years since she had heard from her brother. Maybe it was time to put her energy, and memories, toward those interested in sharing her life.

Dell said, "I got to get back to my place tomorrow, but Grandy and Will can spend a little time and help you." He gave Mr. Winters a thoughtful look. "You planning on taking everybody in?"

"Hell," said the old man as he blew out a breath, "we could use the excitement. We're just a bunch of old folks here, running a few cattle and keeping you and the Double B from going to war over my water." He grinned as he watched the children eat. "She's my only kin and she brought me a whole family."

"We'll do what we can to help you, old man," said Dell.

Annabella eased the youngsters away from the table saying, "Let's let the gentlemen have some food." She put a hand on Patrick's shoulder. "You and the boys carry your dishes and help Morning Flower." She lifted an eyebrow to Toby and Skeeter. The boys scrambled to be helpful, and Dell was again impressed with her ability to supervise the children.

While their guests ate, Henry and his cowpokes unloaded the wagon, and he was pleased at the supplies Annabella had purchased. "It was Dell's idea," she said. "He told me that six extra mouths would be a challenge to your supplies and that a trip to resupply would be inconvenient and lengthy." She said all this as she methodically organized her belongings and the clothing she had purchased for the youngsters.

There was not much other furniture in the cabin gathering room besides the dining table. The children had slowly drifted to the floor and were falling asleep. "Time to get ready for bed," Annabella announced. "Molly, you and Missy visit the privy and when you return, Skeeter, you take your brother. You older boys follow and then everyone will go to bed. You heard Mr. Winters, we have to build a few things tomorrow.

And that's what happened. As the youngsters returned from the privy, Annabella had warm water in a basin at the table and made certain everyone washed. She ushered the girls to the spare bedroom where Morning Flower helped them undress and crawl onto blankets.

Little Byron was happy to snug down with his brother and all the boys were soon under blankets. The men, understanding that it was bedtime, moved out to the bunk house. Mr. Winters disappeared into his room and Annabella found herself alone with Morning Flower. "We'll have a busy day tomorrow. I hope we won't make your life difficult."

Morning Flower looked at her with deep, dark eyes. "It was too quiet before you come. Maybe better now." Annabella touched the squaw's arm in a gentle caress and both women went to bed.

xxx

Even though there were nine people sleeping in the cabin, Annabella heard only soft snorts since she was tucked away in the little bedroom. Henry had prepared a marriage-sized bed for the guest room in anticipation of his son's visit. Tonight Annabella and the two girls were snuggled together on the new mattress. The room held a small table and bureau. It was just large enough that all three of them could prepare for bed without bumping into one another.

In the dark quiet room she reviewed her day, a long dusty train ride, taking in six children, meeting several ranchers and finally coming face to face with Mr. Winters, her father-in-law. It had taken her many years to school herself in emotional control - not showing any signs of distress, disappointment or despair. She hoped she had kept her demeanor under control today. She wasn't certain how she felt about this new circumstance. Through all of her resettlements these last ten years, she might have been lonely, but she was always within a civilized community. Today she had moved to the wild west. It didn't seem too bad - so far. But she was mingling with many different people - Indians, Negroes, Mexican laborers. They appeared to be kind and accepting. Maybe she should follow her own personal rules, stay calm, stay aloof, stay quiet. What she wasn't, was frightened. No one today had caused her to feel panic or suspicion. Maybe the wild west was friendlier than a big city.

But what about the children? This thought did cause some panic! Somehow she was now in a role that was beyond teacher, beyond nanny, and almost mother. She had mothered Chad Winters' son during her brief marriage. She tried to remember what she had learned. Not much. She reviewed the techniques that she learned as a teacher. Maybe mothering six children would be like teaching - except they would never go home at the end of the day. And maybe they would expect affection. Something else to cause panic.

What would her future be with these children? Just having spent one day with them she knew that they needed more than a teacher gave. They needed hugs, and nurturing. They needed laughter, a steady life, food, clothing, shelter. Teachers didn't give all that - teachers gave tutoring, lessons, encouragement. But teachers had private lives. Teachers had privacy and freedom.

She thought about her life over the last ten years - teaching by day, loneliness at night. She had no longtime friendships, no memories of sharing days of fun, no laughter or silliness - all that died when her brother sent her away. For ten years she might have had freedom and privacy, but to her it only meant that she had been very lonely.

Would this be a new and better life? She hadn't had time to find a new life with Mr. Winters before he and his son had died. Was this another chance to live? She looked inside herself. Did she have any affection to share? Any joy? Any interest in building a life with these new people? She looked and looked within herself, and finally cried herself to sleep because she was unable to find herself, the old Annabella, the one who used to know how to laugh and enjoy life.

CHAPTER 4

The next morning the ranch house was abustle at first light. Morning Flower was preparing breakfast and the boys who had been asleep in front of her stove had awakened and were wandering to the privy.

Annabella scrambled from her bed and decided to dress in her ranch clothes. She had purchased work pants and shirts for her and all the children. She had even purchased men's boots for herself. She just hoped in her attempt to be practical she wasn't a spectacle. Appearing in the main room, she quickly saw the fleeting grin on Morning Flowers face. The old woman nodded a good morning, then said, "You ready to work hard."

"I am." Annabella took that as acceptance.

With her schoolroom authority she quickly organized the boys, collecting their old clothes and putting them into the new. Toby, not shy about donning new clothes in front of her, said, "I never had something that Will, I mean Patrick, didn't wear first." He wasn't certain how he looked and Annabella could tell that he needed affirmation. A typical boy, she thought.

She tousled his hair and said, "Mighty fine looking young man." He grinned. "Why don't you run to the bunkhouse and tell the men we're getting breakfast ready?" He was out the door in a flash.

Little Byron was left behind. Annabella helped him into new clothes, washed his face and corralled Molly to take him to the privy. "Now, Byron," she instructed, "you make certain that Molly doesn't lose you. We don't want you to miss breakfast." The solemn boy nodded and clasped Molly's hand.

The young girl grinned at Annabella and mouthed, "He's so cute."

Annabella watched the other two boys gather their new clothing and race to the bunkhouse to find some privacy. As they dashed into the bunkhouse, she decided that later today she should inspect that building to see what opportunities it offered as sleeping space. Standing at the window she watched Dell walk from the bunkhouse to the main house. It was time for her to begin a new life, talk with people, invite friendship, welcome neighbors. "I hope you slept well," she offered, practicing her new persona, as he came through the door.

He nodded and asked, "Coffee?" Morning Flower handed him a steaming cup. After a gulp, he asked, "You have a good sleep?" Annabella nodded as she accepted a cup of coffee from Morning Flower.

"You two eat breakfast before everyone else gets here," ordered Morning Flower who had become more a person this morning than an invisible squaw.

Dell, thinking that Morning Flower had a good idea, grabbed the plate she handed him and took a seat. Annabella sat across the table and attacked her own plate. They heard Henry open his bedroom door and they watched as he walked directly to Morning Flower for his mug of coffee.

After greeting his guests, he announced, "We got a lot to do today. Dell, can you send over some planks so I can get a floor in my loft for those boys?"

"Can they sleep in the bunkhouse?" asked Annabella.

The men exchanged glances, then Dell said, "The older ranch hands won't appreciate being nursemaids. They'll help with the youngsters and teach them, but they like their time alone."

"Besides," Henry added, "I take on extra hands from time to time and need a place for them to bunk."

She nodded. "I understand. I like the boys close to me, but this house is small."

"I think we'll get the loft in for now," said Henry, "and work on adding an extra room in time for winter.

Soon the house was filled with those seeking food and those, like little Byron, who were just trying to remember where they were. Annabella walked Dell out to his horse as he prepared to leave. "I'll send over more blankets and a few other things I think you'll need."

"You've been so kind already," she assured him, "We should stop imposing on your good nature." A part of Annabella encouraged her in the exchange, reminding her that this was the first informal relaxed conversation she may have ever had with a man.

"I won't always be this kind," he told her with a smile. "One of my boys will bring a wagon over later today." In his life as a busy rancher Dell rarely spoke with women. He had a lady friend he visited from time to time, but it wasn't for conversation. Today he was talking with a woman decked out in wrangler clothing who guarded her heart. Hmmm.

Annabella stared at the horizon. "How far is your ranch?"

He stood behind her and pointed over her shoulder to the east. "We crossed a portion of my land when we gained the plateau yesterday. On horseback, the ride is about fifteen minutes to my boundary and then another twenty to the house. Twenty minutes all told if you ride hard. The trail is easy to follow. In a wagon sometimes it takes over an hour depending on the condition of the trail." He looked her up and down, measuring the figure she presented in her men's clothing. It made him interested to know her better. "Do you ride, or can you drive a wagon?"

"I'm better at driving a wagon," she replied. "When I was married, we managed a mercantile and I often made deliveries."

Dell finished saddling his horse. "You might think about taking Morning Flower for a buggy ride now and then. I don't think she's left the ranch since Henry bought her."

"Bought her?" It came out as a screech.

Dell signaled that she should lower her voice. But Annabella was clearly upset and needed more information. "I don't know all the particulars," he said, "but Henry had his two ranch hands and somehow Morning Flower was brought to the ranch by some Indians." He scanned the horizon. "Those hills. They live up in the hills, hiding from government men, and I guess they needed money, or she was too old to keep up that harsh life."

Annabella sputtered unable to find words to express her displeasure.

"Don't you judge," warned Dell, "until you know the whole story. Henry's been real good to her. She was just skin and bones when he got her." He climbed on his horse and looked down at her. "Just wait until you hear the story. Henry talks enough." He tipped his hat to her and cantered away in the direction of his ranch.

When Annabella returned to the house Henry and Will were planning their work for the day. Charlie and Manuel had finished breakfast and were ready to handle routine ranch chores. Charlie looked at Annabella and asked, "These boys, can they work?" He was an interesting looking fellow - dark brown skin stretched over a face that was the very essence of Africa in Annabella's limited experience. He was tall with a graying beard and long calloused fingers. But his eyes were his asset. They brimmed with warmth and affection especially as he helped with the children.

She looked at the three older boys. They wanted to be out around the ranch doing all the exploring that boys do, but they understood they would do what was needed. She smiled at them. "If this were September, they would have to do their schooling first, but it's summertime, so I guess they can learn to help you." The boys cheered.

Charlie looked at Annabella and asked, "When you start that schooling, can you help me to read?" The question startled her, but she smiled softly and nodded.

"Si," said Manuel as he joined the conversation. The Mexican appeared younger than Henry and Charlie, but just as worn and calloused. He was small and wiry with a ready smile for everyone this morning.

The boys looked shocked. "You want to get schooled?" asked Skeeter.

"Don't you want to know all you can so nobody cheats you?" asked Charlie.

The youngster thought about that and asked Annabella. "Will we all study together?"

She smiled to herself but calmly replied, "You'll have to be as serious about learning as the men are. We don't want any distractions." All three boys nodded solemnly. They would be serious students.

With that decided, Charlie signaled for them to follow him out to help with the chores.

Molly materialized at Annabella's side wearing her new cowpoke clothes. "Can I go, too?"

"Morning Flower and I will need help with the house chores and with the two younger children."

Molly scowled. "The boys will have all the fun. They'll ride horses and climb trees."

Annabella remembered those days when she watched her brother play outdoors and she had to stay inside and do chores and learn ladylike things like embroidery and music lessons. "I do want you to learn to ride a horse," she said looking stern. After a moment of thought, she offered, "Why don't you work in the house in the mornings and work outside in the afternoon? At lunch we'll talk to Charlie about the kind of work you can do."

Molly wrestled with the offer. Annabella could see it all on her cute, freckled face. Finally, the youngster agreed. "Outside after lunch. Do you think I'll ride a horse?"

"Maybe not today," said Annabella. "But it is necessary for you to learn if we live on a ranch." Molly liked that idea and ran to find the small children.

By lunch time another table appeared with the necessary benches. It was the same size as the existing table. Henry argued that put together they made one long table so the family could eat together. And Charlie pointed out that the tables could be re-arranged as separate for schooling. Annabella thought they had a very good idea.

Molly moved outdoors after lunch taking her turn on a horse and carrying water for the livestock - three cows, some pigs, several dozen chickens and a burro. As Charlie was heard to comment, "She works harder than those boys and the animals like her better."

Morning Flower even found work for the two smallest children. Byron and Missy were assigned piling rocks. For several years Henry had been collecting rocks pulled from his fields and river bed and surrounding mountains slowly working the rocks into a stone facade on the house. Currently the cabin had a half finished look about it. Henry had built up the corners, slowly filling in the space up the walls. He did additional work as rocks and time allowed. He prophesied that it would be done before he died. Annabella thought the rock facade would create a certain elegant look - once it was finished, of course.

A wagon arrived after lunch with supplies from Dell. It included enough wood for Henry and Will to make a floor and several platforms that they hoisted into the rafters creating the sleeping loft for the children. The boys were especially delighted with the crude ladder the men constructed to access the sleeping space. Skeeter told everyone he felt like he was climbing up to a tower to protect the castle.

Annabella was again reminded why she liked being a teacher; she always enjoyed youth and imagination.

xxx

After completing beds and tables Henry began planning an addition to the cabin. He talked over his idea with Annabella saying, "I think this will be the spot for you. We can keep the girls in the small room, and you can have some place to be alone." They were standing outside behind the fireplace. Henry was proposing that he remove a window and make it a door. In his vision the small addition would give Annabella privacy and a place for her personal belongings.

"That's very thoughtful, Mr. Winters."

"You gonna call me Henry?"

"Yes. You're very thoughtful, Henry."

He seemed to blush. "Now I don't know when I'll get this finished 'cause we got a lot of summer work to do."

"The girls and I will be fine until you have time." She took his hand as they stood staring at the cabin window that would be the doorway to Annabella's room. "I appreciate all that you have done for me and the children already." Showing appreciation for each act of friendship and warmth was a challenge for Annabella. She just hoped Henry understood how grateful she was. She hoped that in time she would find her true warmth, her true self, after all these years of her lifeless existence.

"Me and my squaw like the sound of these youngsters." He seemed to blush again. "Laughing and all that energy." Annabella couldn't resist, she gave him a quick hug.

xxx

Day one, Annabella told herself as she settled into bed. Mr. Winters had worked hard to provide sleeping space for her and the children. She and the two girls had their own small room and the four boys would sleep in the loft of the cabin. Mr. Winters had directed the construction of tables, benches and bunks so that everyone could sit at the table and eat meals together and have a good night's sleep.

He was an interesting man. Annabella suspected that there was a lot more to him than the old rancher appearance that he projected. This evening she thought about the hug she had given him today. She was appalled at her behavior. She couldn't remember the last time she had felt comfortable sharing a hug. Had she hugged her brother when she left Cincinnati? If she had that would have been the last hug - until today. She wondered if she would be so spontaneous again. She had been confused by her action and had excused herself from any more discussion by moving on to other chores.

Morning Flower was a pleasant surprise, she thought. The older woman cooked for seven more people without blinking an eye. She didn't talk much but she smiled and seemed to anticipate everyone's needs. Annabella knew there was sorrow and fear inside this aging Indian squaw. She could see it in the older woman's eyes. But she also saw kindness and a gentleness with the children. Would Morning Flower ever share her story?

Share her story? Annabella shocked herself again. First a hug and now an interest in delving into someone's private life. No colleague in all her years of teaching had ever asked a personal question or shared family anecdotes. In fact, no one even knew the date of Annabella's birthday. Ten years of no acknowledgement. She wondered if that meant she hadn't aged. She poked her pillow, as she thought, now you're getting silly.

But Henry and Morning Flower had stories to share. And just knowing them for one day had Annabella interested in knowing more about them. Does that mean I'm willing to share my story, Annabella asked herself? And the six children had stories she was certain would outline young lives facing uncertainty and hunger. Just one day with the children and she knew she could never part from them. Each one needed affection and kindness. Annabella was certain that their stories would be as scary as Morning Flower's.

Maybe her ten years in purgatory hadn't been as bad as she had thought. The children may have escaped from hell. She yawned.

It was time to sleep.

CHAPTER 5

"This is a big garden," Annabella said to Morning Flower. Each day Annabella learned more about life on the ranch. Cincinnati and St. Louis had been so civilized.

"Winter is long," replied the older woman. "We preserve and store much food."

"Where?" The ranch house was bursting at the seams with people. There didn't seem to be space to spare for winter food. Morning Flower led Annabella to the kitchen area and a corner against the wall between the kitchen and the bedroom. She moved a small table and pointed to a grip coming out of the floor. Pulling and lifting a trapdoor, she climbed into the hole using a small ladder that dropped down into an old root cellar its walls lined with rocks, the same rocks that were being used to cover the outside walls of the cabin.

Annabella followed. She looked around the space. "You can store a lot of food."

"We will smoke some meat and make some jerky in the fall," Morning Flower informed her. "We put up beans and apples and store potatoes and onions. We not go hungry."

They climbed out of the cellar and went back to working in the vegetable garden.

"This is still a lot of food," commented Annabella as she stretched after working a long row of squash.

Morning Flower surveyed the area. "We sell to store in town and to the other ranchers." She studied the acres. "We sell potatoes, squash, peppers, and eggs."

"Eggs?" Annabella had seen the coop leaning against the barn. But it didn't look very productive or organized.

"Ranchers buy eggs to feed cowboys." Morning Flower swung her arm. "They not have time to tend flock. Not all ranchers have wives and daughters to do kitchen work like gardens and chickens. You watch every few days a cook comes to get eggs and other food."

Once Annabella paid attention, she did notice the strangers coming with large straw filled boxes and leaving with supplies. Exploring the coop she found that it was much bigger than she had first thought. And when she got closer she met a large dog who seemed to be on guard duty.

"That's Jeffry," announced Molly bouncing into the chicken yard. "He guards the chickens at night so no animals come to steal them."

"Is he a friend of yours?" Annabella studied the thin, bright youngster. Molly was always eager to work outside every afternoon.

"Oh, yes," the young girl said proudly. "He doesn't like the boys. They want him to do tricks. He likes me because I scratch his ears." She pushed the dog aside and placed water and scattered feed for the chickens. Once she had emptied the small basket of corn she began to hunt through the nests for eggs.

Annabella smiled and scratched the dog's ears while Molly praised each hen as she carefully placed eggs in her basket.

Each day Annabella found more to notice and absorb. Today she learned that Molly had names for each hen!

xxx

One day Annabella realized she had a problem. Bathing. Even in her simple life with her husband, there had been a bath closet in the rooms above the mercantile. There was nothing at the ranch that she had found. And the more she thought about washing, the grittier she felt. After all, she gardened each day, supervised six children, helped cook, bake the daily bread, and cleaned up the cabin. Several times a day she washed her face and hands. In her small room, that she shared with the girls, she might manage a quick rinse from the waist up before being called to some crisis.

Would she ever be clean again? And the children - they needed more than a swipe across their cheeks and a dash over their hands to be clean. Wasn't cleanliness next to godliness? Was she raising little devils? She would solve this problem. But first she had to stop and scratch - she was certain she had lice in her hair. She just wanted to scrub!

Then came the next logical question - clean clothes! If there was no place to bathe, was there some place to wash clothing? Annabella puzzled that question. Henry and the ranch hands seemed to wear the same shirt every day. And after a week here at the ranch, she could smell the shirts. Her mind almost melted at the thought of six children never wearing clean clothing and never bathing. Cities had so many more conveniences than a ranch did. She had never washed her own clothing. During her years as a teacher that service was always included as part of the fees for the rooming house. When she married Mr. Winters, he had told her he hired a washer woman. He wanted Annabella's help in the store. She wouldn't have time to do laundry.

She itched and she was certain her clothing smelled of sweat and dirt and dogs and chickens. She almost moaned aloud.

Looking up at a shouted greeting, she saw the solution to her problems. Dell, her instructor on all things ranch, was riding into the yard. She jumped to her feet, dusted at least today's layer of dirt from her clothing and greeted him. "I need some advice."

Dell leaned over his saddle and grinned, "Yes ma'am." He always looked forward to conversations with Annabella.

She blushed and he was charmed. He wondered what was troubling this very proper lady. Lowering her voice, she said, "Let's take a walk and I'll tell you my problem."

Several concerns popped into his head, a fight with Henry, one of the kids was causing trouble, maybe one of the ranch hands got uppity. He followed her as she led him away from the house and barn.

Once she determined they could not be heard she turned to him and whispered, "Dell, I need a bath." Her eyes held a plea, her lips were tight in a straight line. This was serious to Annabella.

He nodded to the stream that flowed by. "That's the ranch bathing room."

She gasped. "I WANT A BATH!"

He guessed his solution wasn't what she wanted to hear. With a stifled laugh, he shouted back at the house, "Henry, you still got that tub?" The old man came out of the cabin, found Dell and waved in the direction of the tool shed. Dell turned Annabella in that direction. "Come on."

When they got to the shed, he explained, "Henry is a one for buying things he might need. He likes ordering from those catalog folks." He unlatched the door and invited Annabella to look inside. Henry had certainly been shopping.

"A washing apparatus! A bathing tub! A sewing machine!" She spun around in delight. "He bought these things?"

"Henry likes to tinker," explained Dell. "Once he figures it out and if his squaw or hands don't want it, he puts it here." They looked into the dark corners of the shed. "No telling what you'll find."

"I've found enough for now." She gave him a soft restrained smile. She was not used to sharing her feelings, no matter how simple. The smile vanished. "Do you think Henry would mind if I moved the bathing tub to my room. I so want to be clean."

Dell pushed aside some contraption and lifted the tub. "Let's take it up and see if it fits in your room. You'll have to carry in the water. And the kids may want to watch."

She stumbled as she thought about entertaining the children with her bath. "They .. I -"

"I think you can use this as a teaching opportunity." Dell so enjoyed her blush.

Soon everyone had gathered to watch Dell carry the strange thing into the house. Once he set it in the middle of the floor, Annabella was bombarded with questions. Predictably, the girls were ready for a bath. Neither had ever enjoyed something so luxurious. And the boys respectfully declined. Byron was torn. He liked the idea of sitting in a large tub of water, but he was reluctant to do it naked.

"We are all going to be clean," stated Annabella. No one argued. Even the ranch hands held their tongues. "The girls will bathe in the tub and you boys may bathe in the stream. I'm certain we can find a safe pool where you can all soap up and get clean." They all looked at Byron. "Patrick," Annabella continued, "if Byron joins you boys, you are responsible for his safety, and Skeeter you are responsible for his washing. If he chooses the tub, I will be responsible for those things." The journey to a soapy salvation began.

xxx

Everyone was finally clean, sighed Annabella as she sank into the bed she shared with Missy and Molly. Finding that bathing tub had been her salvation. What a luxury to soak in soapy water for almost ten minutes and to wash her hair. It had been almost three weeks.

Once she and Dell had found the tub, he had carried it into her bedroom followed by six curious kids. The boys helped carry water from the spring house, a little diversionary rivulet running through a small shelter Henry had fashioned to store butter and eggs. "Do we have to bathe?" asked a suspicious Skeeter.

"I'll think about it," murmured Annabella as she stared longingly at the slowly filling tub. She thought she heard Dell laugh. Once the water stood four inches she was ready. Morning Flower dashed in with a kettle of boiling water emptying it into the tub. "Thank you," gushed the eager bather. She pushed everyone from the room and latched the door, saying, "I'll call if I need anything." Did Dell laugh again?

When she opened the door, Annabella was surprised to find Molly waiting. "I would like to try that," she hinted, casting an eye toward the tub.

"Where are the boys?"

"Dell said men bathed in the river. Women bathed in tubs. He took them there." She sidled into the room and waited to be instructed on bathing like a woman. Annabella smiled to herself.

"Let's get some more warm water and find another bathing towel." She was wrapped in her sleeping robe and had combed her wet hair and tied it at the back of her neck. She called to Morning Flower and searched the kitchen for more towels.

When she returned to the bedroom, she found Molly naked waiting for further instructions while Missy was quickly disrobing. Annabella instructed Molly on washing, helped her scrub her hair and wrapped her into a towel. Missy needed no coaxing and soon settled into the tub as Morning Flower added some warm water from the kettle. Annabella washed the little girl's hair and helped her scrub her ears and her feet. For each girl she added some soap flakes from her precious supply of feminine products. Who knew when she would find a new supply of delicate soaps again?

The three of them enjoyed the all-girl time with new scents and drying hair. There was a scratch at the door. Missy opened it and a naked Byron popped into the room. "Tub," he said as he pointed. They laughed and Annabella helped him into the tub. The girls helped him wash and showed him how the fragrant soap made bubbles. They washed his hair and scrubbed his fingers and toes.

Before dinner everyone gathered at the cabin. The boys were clean and fresh smelling with Dell's assistance. The girls and Byron were clean and scented with Annabella's help. Dell and Patrick carried the tub out to empty in the garden. Morning Flower gave everyone a slice of buttered bread and they all talked about this new adventure.

"We never had a bathing tub," said Molly.

"How did you get clean?" Annabella was curious. She hadn't found crusted dirt on the girls or Byron.

"Mama had a pail and she would make us stand in it - one person each night and she washed us," explained Toby. "Patrick was big, so he went with Pop to the barbershop tent."

Annabella looked at Dell, confused. He explained, "In the mining camps the barber tent was sort of a bathing house for the men. You pay a few cents, and you could stand under a spout and the water came over you and you washed."

"When Pap and I went we had to stand together because we didn't have enough money for two washes," explained Patrick. "We had to be quick because they only let a little bit of water come through the pipes for each person."

"Wow," said Skeeter. "I don't remember any bathing. When dad came home, he yelled at the lady with us if we were dirty. They always made sure our hands and faces were clean. On warm days I played in the river. So I guess I was clean."

Patrick popped the last of his buttered bread into his mouth and asked, "What do we do with those?"

They all turned to look at the pile of dirty clothes by the door. "Tomorrow we learn how to do laundry," announced Annabella. The boys groaned.

CHAPTER 6

Henry drove his wagon into town every nine or ten days. He sold eggs and chickens to the general store. He also sold vegetables when they ripened and fruit from his trees. Morning Flower made butter and an interesting Indian cheese that he also sold. If Annabella didn't go along, he took Patrick or Toby to teach them to drive the wagon. He was teaching Patrick how to drive the wagon so that he could take produce and eggs to the other ranchers on the plateau.

Annabella soon learned that what she wanted didn't compare to what she needed. She frequently joined Henry on his trips to town. One of the children always needed shoes or longer trousers. They grew so fast. And when September arrived she would have to purchase warm clothing, mittens, jackets and all manner of garments she and the children would need for the winter that Henry was predicting.

To her surprise Henry often paid for the children's supplies, saying, "I got a mighty fine family and I want them to stay warm," or "well fed," or "they need some candy today." Annabella always smiled and gave him a quick hug.

Through her trips into town she was getting to know local folks. The minister, a banker and the man at the mercantile where books arrived via the mail. She always found a minute to chat with the local teacher to exchange ideas.

Annabella was never lonely and never bored in her new life. The house was organized, the children had chores, Morning Flower was smiling, and Henry loved each child as if he or she were his own. And the ranch hands were slowly constructing an addition on the back side of the cabin's fireplace. By Christmas Henry promised that she would have her own room. What more could she want?

xxx

Summer was in full swing and Annabella had found a quiet spot where she sat in the evening to daydream and think about daily ranch life. One evening Henry found her sitting under a tree at the edge of the garden, the next day he had built a comfortable bench with a slatted back for her. Now her evenings were spent in comfort as she enjoyed the silence and the stars while she thought about her day and her many small inter-actions with the adults and children.

Dell usually arrived after dinner to inspect the work of the day and to see if more help was needed. He always reminded her that he had prom-ised to see that she and the children were taken care of and had what they needed. Annabella had laughed at him. "We have more than we need, especially the attention and interest Henry and the ranch hands lavish on these children."

"Just like fertilizer on a crop," Dell observed.

"You're a cowpoke philosopher, Dell." She gave him a coy tilt of her head. Then stopped. Was she flirting? She had never done that in her life. Was she finding that young Annabella, the one who laughed?

And that was life for Annabella and the children for the summer - building, growing and frequent visits from Will and Dell.

xxx

Annabella was taking Skeeter and Molly into town with Henry one day. The children always needed something. Skeeter had no idea of his age, but he seemed to be growing at a fast rate recently. Overnight he seemed

44

to grow inches. Annabella was carefully storing his old clothing for Byron. She smiled. Little Byron would take years to grow into those clothes.

A teacher never had to worry about these things, but now that she was their guardian, and maybe almost their mother, she had to pay attention to other aspects of the youngsters' lives. Today Skeeter needed shoes and longer trousers. Molly needed shoes. She was growing into a young lady, but she didn't seem interested in the other refinements of girlhood.

However, she surprised Annabella when they arrived at the mercantile. "Miss Annabella," the youngster chirped, "look at these ribbons. Missy and I don't have any ribbons. We could put them in our hair." She held the pinkest ribbon along her cheek.

Annabella smiled at her. "I think it's just the right color." She enjoyed using all the money she had saved over the years to take care of the children's needs. And sometimes she enjoyed spending it on their dreams.

Skeeter quickly selected his trousers so that he had time to look over the toys and candy. "Miss Annabella," he called, "there's a new candy." He rattled a colorful tin. "It's from Philadelphia. Maybe Byron would like to try it."

"We can only purchase it if you think there are enough pieces for all the children," she cautioned him. He rattled the tin.

The store manager said, "Miss Annabella, I have more tins. I've one here behind the counter that you can see and, maybe sample." She had become his best customer since her arrival that day at the depot.

She sampled the gooey, minty treat, counted the pieces in the tin. "I think we'll need three." The man gave her a solemn nod and added them to her other purchases.

Henry popped into the store and called out, "Did you get my supplies?" She nodded. "Then we can return home. I sold all my goods."

The kids moaned because a day in town was never long enough for them, but they helped carry the packages to the wagon.

xxx

Annabella liked the evenings after dinner. There was a calming rhythm as the ranch was put to bed. The older children had chores to do and often Dell and Will came by for a visit. They lived on a plateau about a thousand feet above the valley. This evening she asked Dell about the history of the plateau. There were five ranches on about ten thousand acres of rolling land divided by several tributaries finally forming a small river that tumbled toward the edge of the escarpment and down toward the town.

"How did you find this place?" she asked.

Dell scuffed his boot against the porch edge. He had found her sitting on the porch enjoying the sunset. "My parents came here right after the war and after the army had fought the Indians. They were looking for a place they could live and feed us. They had come from some poverty in the east." He stared out across the farmyard. "We have an uncle in St. Louis, my father's brother. That's about all the family they stayed connected to." He watched the sky flare out into night. "They made us a good life here. Two other families came with them and they shared the land. Then the government came in and wanted everyone to have boundaries. By that time we had another two ranchers. Everyone got a share. Henry got the smallest piece but it protects the headwaters so no one dams the streams. Some of us are more prosperous than others."

"I haven't met any of the families, have I?"

"Only two of the ranches have families, you know wives and youngsters. Us and Henry and Billy at the Double B are all bachelors. Our ranch is the biggest, but me and Will work hard. We have about a dozen hands. Double B has the same, but his crew doesn't work as hard as our guys. They have reputations for going into town and causing trouble. I think the other two ranchers struggle some to make a profit. But being a ranch, they have food for their families. And maybe that's all they need. Will and I would like to buy them out some day."

"Who is this Billy at Double B? I've never heard Henry mention him."

"He's the one closest to me and Henry, a lousy rancher and a mean son of a - I mean a hard man to deal with."

She grinned at him. "I have heard that sort of language before, Dell. But thank you for keeping it from Byron." The youngster had crawled onto her lap, eyes wide listening to the conversation. "Are you and Will so prosperous that you can buy people out?"

"We're working on it. We save our money and we try to improve our operation and raise stock folks want to buy." He reached over and tweaked Byron's nose. The youngster grinned and burrowed into Annabella. "When we met you Will had just come back from Denver. He sold some stock, bought some breeders and got us a contract to deliver some horses and cattle to the railroad."

"Morning Flower said Henry sells food to everyone."

"He's mighty successful, too," said Dell. "He provides chickens for the restaurant in town and eggs for ranchers. He's probably got requests for Christmas hams from some of the loftier families in town."

"Loftier?" she teased.

He hung his head. "It's no secret, the folks in town think we're all heathen out here on the plateau. None of us gets to church much, or summer dances and gatherings."

Annabella thought about what she had heard. "I guess I don't know very much about this activity - ranching and grazing and livestock."

"You'll learn because you live it now. That's how we all learned."

CHAPTER 7

Annabella was working out in the vegetable garden. Each afternoon she found time to weed and water and pull a few items for supper. Henry wandered into the patch. He wiped his brow with an old handkerchief and placed his hat back on his head. "Today woudda been my son's birthday," he stated as an introduction.

Annabella smiled at him as she stood and rubbed her back. "I know. We had been married two months by this date. We had a small celebration." She also used a handkerchief to wipe her cheeks. Her cloth had once had lace and some embroidery. She smiled thinking about how the cloth that had become so useful as it lost its frills. "His son, Adam, and I baked a cake and kept it in the store. We offered small pieces to our customers that day and each one wished Chad a happy birthday. I think he enjoyed all the attention that day."

"He was mighty shy," said Henry.

"He was, but very considerate and warm." Annabella studied Henry. "Was that your doing?"

The old man laughed. "It was his mama." Henry moved on. Daylight was for work not talk.

xxx

"Byron," moaned Missy, "You have to learn to tie your boots. Watch me." When she finished Missy had made a knotted mess of the boot strings.

Toby had been watching this exercise and laughed. "You can't tie shoes."

"Yes, I can," his sister cried. "It's his feet. They move."

Will, who could never resist a young girl's tears, said, "Let me show you." He unknotted the strings, tucked Byron's toes in snuggly and promptly knotted the laced. "Damn."

"Will said damn," called Missy.

"He moved his feet."

Toby laughed harder.

Byron cried.

Molly walked into the cabin. "Oh, Byron sweetie, don't cry. Who hurt you?"

"Shoes." He wiggled his untied shoes, snug on his feet.

Molly sat on the floor pulled him into her lap, reached around and tied his laces. Byron hopped up and ran out the door.

"How'd you do that?" asked Will.

"You have to hold him down or he moves his feet," she said.

Toby sprawled on the floor laughing. Will whomped him with a broom.

xxx

That evening Henry sat at the table, peeled an apple for Byron and said, "Let me finish my story, Miss Annabella." The children gathered close. They loved Henry's stories. "Today would be my son's birthday. He was a fine boy and a good man. When I went off to the war my wife was pregnant. Five years later I returned and I had a son." Tears gathered in his eyes. He swiped at them with his handkerchief. "When I left her, we were heirs to two prosperous plantations in Georgia. When I returned I found her and our son living with Charlie and his wife. The four of them was all that was left."

"Our Charlie?"

"Oh, yes," nodded Henry. "We've been together since my daddy bought his family fifty years ago. And he's been a truer friend than any other man I ever known."

"How did you both get here?"

"Some good luck after all that bad of the war." He tilted his head toward the old black man. "When I got back to Georgia and found what was left and learned what we lost, I talked to my wife and to Charlie and we made a plan. Charlie had buried some gold that my father gave him and some jewelry we could sell. We packed up our wives and children. Charlie and his wife had two. We got out of the place as fast as we could because we didn't want anyone to lay claim to our gold and jewelry."

He nodded at the memory. "There were all kinds of shenanigans going on. We decided to make for Kansas. We found an abandoned farm and began our life." He chortled at the memory. "My wife had been raised as a princess. Even after five years, she hadn't learned much, Charlie's wife had seen to her care. But my wife was smart, so like you, Miss Annabella, she began teaching the children. We all worked hard and built two small homes. Once our farm started to look prosperous the folks who had given it up came by and demanded that we pay them." Now he laughed. "We looked at them and at all we would give up. My wife said, 'Do you want to live near people like them?' We agreed with her and packed up."

"Charlie and I found jobs and we kept moving west. My wife was real smart and as we traveled west, she started studying the papers and the politics and convinced us that we could get this here land. And she was correct. We bought this land in a government sale. Dell's family and Double B were already here, but I was a veteran because I had done a little work for the US Cavalry when we left Kansas.

"The US Cavalry?" asked a puzzled Annabella.

Henry nodded. "They were training some Negro men, former slaves, and they thought I could help." He grinned. "Me and Charlie helped with training. But we wanted to get back with our families. My wife had learned about land grants and showed someone I was a veteran from the cavalry and got my bid accepted for some land. We didn't know that the government men didn't want either of those farmers, Dell's folks or Double B, to own this piece because of the water rights. They wanted a neutral party to keep the place from water wars. We were too dumb to know."

"But why?" Annabella wondered if the water discussion was related to the statehood talk she had heard when she first arrived. But it was almost bedtime, not time to talk politics.

Charlie spoke up. "When we got here, there was still a fort close by." Everyone nodded because Dell had pointed it out the day they arrived on the plateau. "They used us to protect the fort's water supply until they closed the place." Henry nodded as Charlie continued. "Those folks at the fort worried that either rancher would dam the water and charge the army. Them generals figured Henry and me was too dumb to do that."

"We built this house and started Charlie's place but his wife died. So he said he was happy with a smaller place. By that time his two youngsters had left us and moved further west. Chad was still with us and he was learning to be a farmer. But it wasn't something he liked. He was a dreamer. His mother's boy. He left us to improve his schooling. One day he returned with his wife and my grandson. They told us they were living in Colorado and we had a good visit and they promised to stay in touch. My wife died and he came to help bury her. Then he went back to his wife and son, but always had a letter once a month for me. He was a good son and said that he wouldn't worry as long as me and Charlie were together. We were left to ourselves, two old men, and we were making friends here. So we stayed."

Annabella patted his shoulder. "Chad was very kind and I think he got some of that from you. Look how you took us in and how you enjoy each of the children."

"Me and my wife wanted more, but..." Henry had no language to tell another woman about his wife's health. "My son wrote to me and said that you were a fine woman. I guess that's why we get on."

CHAPTER 8

Over the long summer nights, Henry usually told stories, about the war, about ranching about people he had met. Annabella always chuckled to herself. Henry's stories had their basis in mythology and Latin translations of Caesar's campaigns. But the children bought every word.

Patrick listened to Charlie and Henry talk about their exploits and how they had arrived at the ranch. They had survived the war that divided the states. They had traveled west and manned the forts as settlers moved from the east to find new homes and create new towns. They struggled and always triumphed. Patrick felt he had been through a war, too - just keeping the family together, working and watching his parents struggle and die. And one night it was his turn to tell a story.

"How'd you get here?" Henry asked the red headed boy who had grown almost as big as any man. "You heard my story." He handed Patrick the end piece of bread. It was another evening after a long day of working the ranch. Annabella always gave everyone a slice of bread and warm milk before bed. Patrick admitted to himself that ranch work was easy because he didn't have to worry. He didn't have to face the challenges and the treachery of the months before they found Miss Annabella.

The youngster surveyed his siblings sitting around the great room. He had never told the girls the entire story. Toby had been so frightened that he couldn't bring himself to frighten the girls, too. "Our pop died in a mine cave-in in a town near Denver. I don't know how it happened. It was his job. We lived in the camp."

"In a shanty," added Toby. "It was smelly and horrible. Mom tried to keep it clean."

"We went to school when we could," said Molly.

"When Pop died," Patrick took over again, "Mom had to take in laundry. A sickness went through the camp. She took to her bed. Toby and I got jobs. Molly and Missy took care of Mom."

"We had to quit school," said Molly. Missy moved closer to her sister and buried her face.

"Mama died," said the little girl.

"Toby and I came home from work and found the neighbor lady helping some men take mama away. She told us she would help us, but we would have to pay her to stay in the shanty."

"She said it was hers," offered Toby.

"But she said we could go back to school," said Molly.

Patrick took a deep breath. "Toby and I kept our jobs, and the girls went to school. But I didn't like them home without us. So Toby left his job and went to school and watched the girls. One day we got home and everything was gone. The lady had taken all that we had."

"Our mom's clothes and Pop's things and the two books we had and our blankets."

"Even my dolly," cried Missy.

The adults in the room hung their heads, embarrassed by the thieving behavior of some unknown swindler. "She probably sold everything," said Charlie.

Patrick nodded. "That's what we learned. One of the other neighbors told us to leave before some people found us and put us in an orphanage. We only had my wages because I never left our money at home. I always carried it in my shoe. We went to the depot and tried to remember where we had lived before the shanty. We knew we had an uncle. But we didn't know where. We saw the kids on the train and a man said if we got on, we didn't have to pay, and someone would meet us."

Patrick blushed. "I guess I didn't understand what he meant. The other kids on the train explained what would happen. At each station people would look us over and pick those they thought would work hard. They said we would be separated."

"So we came up with a plan," explained Toby.

"Mama always said Toby was our planner," said Molly. "Papa said he would be a general one of these days."

Henry nodded and patted the youngster on the back. "A strategic thinker."

"What's that?" asked Skeeter.

"That's someone who looks at the problem and figures out how to solve it," said Annabella. She was surprised she could speak on such a neutral topic because she was close to tears.

"So, Missy found Miss Annabella and we followed Toby's plan." Patrick finished his story.

"What was your plan?" asked Henry, thinking a lot had been left out of the explanation.

Toby grinned at his audience. "We sent Missy around the train to find a lady traveling alone. When she got off, we would, too, and pretend we were with her."

"But you might have gotten someone who would not be like Annabella," challenged Henry.

"We didn't plan on finding someone as nice as Miss Annabella," said Molly. "We just planned to get off the train with her and then we would figure out our next step."

"We still had Patrick's money," added Toby. "We all decided not to eat for a few days and save it." The girls nodded.

Patrick took over again. "I knew I could work and so could Toby. If we could find a place to stay, the girls could go to school and we would pretend we were waiting for our parents to arrive." He stretched out his arms. "You see how big I am. Folks woudda believed I was old enough to tend to us all for a while." Everyone nodded in agreement.

Annabella took a deep breath and silently sent up thanks that the children had been lucky. She was frightened to think about what evils could have happened to them.

"Wow," said Skeeter. "I didn't have any plan. Our mama put us on the train and told me to look after Byron. She said our pop would meet us." A tear ran down his cheek. "But on the train I heard what the other kids said and knew she lied to us. I don't think she was our real mama. Our pop always had different women cooking and staying with us. He would go off for days and the lady would take care of us. One of the ladies left Byron and didn't come home. Pop just brought another lady and never said anything. He left again but didn't come home for weeks. That's when she put us on the train and lied to us."

He looked at his audience. "We don't even know our other name."

"But you went to school," said Annabella, "you know how to read."

"I just went when I could," he explained, "if they needed another name no one ever said." He shrugged. "Maybe they knew my pop and knew what my name was."

"Shit," said Manuel. "After those stories, I got nothing to complain about." The others nodded.

Henry walked up behind Skeeter and put a hand on his shoulder. "Your other name is now Winters." The boy grinned. Byron was asleep in Charlie's lap.

xxx

Annabella had easily fashioned a routine for life on the ranch. Mornings were devoted to chores - cleaning, cooking, laundry and working the garden. After lunch she worked on personal tasks. She had to laugh, personal meant taking apart her clothing and fashioning useful items. She made draperies from her travel dress for the few windows in the cabin. Today she was working in her small bedroom, making blouses for the girls out of her two best summer dresses. No buttons just serviceable smocks that she could gather at the neck and cuffs with ribbons. Molly had complained that she needed something that felt like she was a girl. Ruefully Annabella had to admit that the girl would soon be a young woman.

In the process of salvaging fabric, Annabella was assembling scraps to begin a quilt for the winter and maybe fashion a doll for Missy. As she worked she saw Byron wander through the house clutching a small blan-

55

ket. This was his nap time. He liked to find Annabella in her quiet workspace. He spread his blanket on the floor by her feet and napped. It was something she enjoyed. The pleasure of the quiet room and the resting child reassured her that coming to live with Henry had been a good decision.

She stared at the little boy and smiled as she thought of his sweetness. He managed to always find arms to hold him and a lap to balance on. And every evening when she tucked him in, he clasped his little arms around her neck for a fierce hug. It was a beautiful way to end every day.

Her reverie was interrupted as Molly and the chicken dog came dashing into the house. "Miss Annabella," she called, "can I ride over to Dell's with Patrick?" The dog sniffed out Byron and gave him a good lick on the cheek. "Can I?"

"May I," corrected Annabella.

"Me, too," said Byron.

Annabella smiled at the two of them. She was doing a lot of that lately. "Molly, you may go with Patrick, just remember to wear your hat. Byron, you stay with me and we'll see if Morning Flower needs any help with dinner."

The boy nodded. He always nodded. Life for Byron seemed to be hugs and smiles. He was content. He pushed the chicken dog off his blanket and gathered it in his arms. "Cook." The dog yipped at that suggestion. Molly dashed off for her adventure and Byron and the dog went to help Morning Flower.

Annabella gathered her piece work and, still smiling, walked into the kitchen to save Morning Flower from Byron's help.

xxx

It had become a habit for Dell to visit most evenings after dinner. He and Annabella would stroll in the garden and sit for the evening on her garden bench. Neither one of them seemed to notice that these visits had become a frequent habit. Everyone else seemed to notice and smile about the budding relationship. And everyone wondered when Dell and Annabella would figure it out. "The children finally told us their stories the other night." Annabella gave a shudder. "I can't get rid of my fear."

"Fear?" asked Dell.

"After I heard them talk, I worried all night about what might have happened." Annabella hung her head and Dell took her hand. "Then I started to worry about all the children on the train that we didn't rescue." She sniffed trying to hide a tear and Dell continued to hold her hand, wanting to put an arm around her and pull her to his chest. But as much as he ached to hold her and chase away her sorrow, he knew that wasn't the gentlemanly thing to do.

"I think you should concentrate on the six we saved," he said softly. To his surprise she rested her head on his shoulder.

They sat in silence for a while, then Annabella began to speak. "I was twenty when my brother put me on a train and sent me away. I was frightened even though I had a destination and people who were meeting me." She raised her head. "But I was as much of an orphan as these children are, only somewhat more fortunate. I had shelter, food and my own money. But since that day I've had no family."

Dell cradled her work-hardened hand in both of his. "You got a mighty big family now."

She gave him one of her rare deep smiles.

xxx

Annabella was just closing down the cabin for the night. She was usually the last one to bed, after making certain the children were all tucked in. As she walked back to her room, she heard voices. The boys were talking in the loft. Patrick whispered, "Is Byron OK?"

"Yeah," Skeeter rasped. "He sometimes dreams he's lost."

She heard crying. Skeeter rasped again, "I can't settle him tonight."

"I'll help," said Patrick. She could hear them shuffling overhead. "He's mighty tiny."

"We ain't had food regular until we got here."

"Us, too," whispered Toby.

"He's quiet now," whispered Patrick. "He just put his hand on my shirt and went to sleep."

"He used to have a rag. I think it was a blanket once. But we lost it with everything else." Skeeter moved above Annabella's head. "He looks OK."

"Do you think we can stay here a while?" Skeeter's voice floated out of the loft.

"I think Miss Annabella and Mr. Henry will care for us," said Toby.

"If not," said Patrick, "We'll take care of you and Byron. We'll all stay together."

Annabella brushed a tear. The children had courage. She loved each one dearly.

CHAPTER 9

After dinner Annabella and Henry sat enjoying the sounds of the new family on a fresh smelling warm evening. Manuel had a guitar and was teaching Toby a song. Charlie was teaching the two smaller children a game with a pebble. Morning Flower was talking with Molly and Skeeter who were both curious about the local Indians. At first she couldn't find Patrick, but finally noticed him leaning against a rail fence, studying the horizon.

"That boy carried a lot of worry before he got here," observed Henry.

"I hope we've made his life easier," she replied.

"We have." Henry scraped and worried his old pipe. She could tell that something was on his mind. "If you've a mind," he began, "I'd like to hear about my son and grandson. I hadn't seen them for three years."

Although she had lived with Mr. Winters and his son for almost a year, what had she learned, what could she say? "He was a very kind man, well-read and intelligent." She smiled at Henry. "He didn't have your handy skills."

Henry laughed. "He couldn't hammer a nail, but he did well with numbers and getting jobs done."

She nodded. "Our store was neat and organized. He dealt kindly with the customers, not fretting over what folks owed. But he managed to keep most accounts even and up to date. Folks in the town respected him."

"What about the boy?" There was a sadness in Henry's voice that reflected his loss.

"He was as good a man as his father." She reached out to touch Henry's arm. "But, now that I've met you I can see that the youngster had some of you in him." Henry looked at her, delighted with that knowledge. She continued, "He had your eyes and sometimes when you stop to think you hold your head the same way he did. And he was more handy than his father. We relied on him to do repairs and to assemble items for display." She became quiet as she reflected on the two men she had lived with and the two men she had not gotten to know as well as she should. Even living together had they all been lonely?

"The boy wanted to come live on the ranch when he got older. He told me he wanted to have animals and help me farm. This would have been his." Henry looked at the children who now lived with him. "I guess I just got me my next generation."

That evening as she couldn't find sleep Annabella thought about her marriage. She had cooked and cleaned for Mr. Winters and his son. She ineptly participated in the marriage bed. She worked side by side with the man in the mercantile. But had she been a good wife? To her the answer was simple. She had failed. She never gave animation to her activities. She worked and slept beside a man and never learned his dreams or his worries. And she never opened her mind and heart to him.

It was a startling truth. She had never opened herself, nor cared to learn more about her husband. Maybe all those years of being alone had withered her. Or maybe through all those years, she had failed at being a possible friend and neighbor, choosing isolation for herself. Had she let opportunities for warmth and sharing pass her by because she didn't know how to initiate friendship?

She stayed very still thinking about her past behavior. Had she made her own loneliness, expecting folks to take her in, entertain her? When, instead, she could have been the one to entertain, to befriend. Was this an opportunity, here at the ranch, her new life, to take control, to befriend, to embrace, to reach out, instead of waiting for life to come to her? Big thoughts to ponder, she thought, and promptly fell asleep.

XXX

Today Annabella was going into town with Patrick and Byron. She liked that combination because Byron had a tendency to wander off. Patrick could be trusted to watch him. When they arrived Henry said, "Looks like that medicine vendor is in town today." Annabella saw a colorful wagon with a platform attached to the back. Several folks were gathered there listening to a man talk about his products.

Both Patrick and Byron were interested in the medicine wagon. Annabella raised an eyebrow and Patrick swallowed his request to visit the wagon. "Let's do your shopping," she said, "then you boys can go around town while Henry and I do our other business." The boy nodded. He helped Byron down from the wagon and followed Annabella into the store.

"Miss Annabella," greeted the store man. "And two growing boys." He sized up Patrick and asked, "New shoes?"

"Mr. Purdy, we need shoes for both boys and then I have a list for things the others at the ranch need." She fished a scrap of paper from her pocket. The boys were dispatched quickly with Byron grasping a candy cane as they ran from the store. Annabella was always puzzled as to how Byron was always understood without saying anything. Well, maybe a word or two - but everyone knew what he wanted.

She finished her shopping and then stopped at the bank to make a withdrawal. Supporting six children was requiring that she manage her funds with more skill than she had needed as a spinster teacher.

Finished with all her errands she went looking for the boys. She knew they would be at the medicine wagon. And there they were. Byron perched in Patrick's shoulders watching the vendor mesmerize the audience with tales of the magic of his elixir. Byron was still sucking his candy cane and it looked to Annabella as though he had gotten it tangled in Patrick's hair. She tried not to laugh as she watched Patrick try to untangle the candy without dropping the small boy. They twisted and juggled. Patrick winced as Byron pulled the candy. More fidgeting. Soon they were attracting more attention than the salesman who shouted, "Hey, you. This is my spot. Go find your own corner."

Annabella didn't understand until she saw that people were laughing at Patrick's predicament and were dropping coins into a small box at his feet. Byron, who seemed to understand their entertainment value, laughed and waved at the folks in the crowd. He pulled his candy cane. Patrick jumped, winced and bobbled the little boy. To her surprise, she watched as Henry stepped in front of the boys, saying, "If you want what makes this fellow so spritely, it's my special Indian squaw tea." He held up a small pouch. "I only got three bags left." Several people waved their arms in interest. The vendor leaped from his wagon charging at Henry. It became mayhem. Henry and the vendor exchanged slugs and were soon rolling around the ground punching and swearing. The crowd enjoyed every minute of the impromptu match, cheering Henry, the hometown favorite.

When the boys were pushed to the edge of the crowd, Annabella grabbed Byron off Patrick's shoulders. "Ouch," he yelled as the boy with the candy and a good-sized knot of hair was pulled into her arms.

She whispered, "Get Henry out of there."

Pushing through the crowd, grabbing Henry by the seat of the pants, Patrick pulled the old man away from the medicine man, tossed Henry over his shoulder and carried him down an alley with Annabella close behind. Henry complained, "I had buyers for my tea. You left good money back there."

Patrick dropped him to the ground and grinned, "I didn't leave my money." He held up the little box with a few coins. Annabella pushed them out of sight of the medicine show crowd. Byron still clutched his candy. She took it from him and dropped it into the weeds. Then she dug out her handkerchief, dipped it in a rain barrel and washed the youngster who seemed to have green sugary candy streaks all over his face and hands.

"Let's get back to the wagon," she ordered, wondering how Henry could cause as much trouble as Byron. "We should leave here before more people notice us." The men moaned.

"I want to sell my tea," argued Henry. He rubbed his eye. It would be black and blue tomorrow.

"Candy," cried Byron.

Patrick opened his mouth with a complaint, but one look from Annabella and he said, "Yes, ma'am."

She got them back to the wagon, dropped Byron on Henry's lap in the wagon bed among the supplies and said, "Patrick, you drive." One last glare from her and no one said a word until they were out of town.

That evening as she related the story to Dell, he laughed. One glare from her and he stopped. But later that evening he entertained Will with Annabella's shopping day adventure.

XXX

Annabella couldn't believe they had been living with Henry for two months. The children were growing and seemed to enjoy their new lives. Charlie and Manuel were patient and kind, helping each one learn new chores and always ready to spin outrageous tales in the evening. Dinners were joyous. Annabella was certain no one noticed that they ate the same meals every day, because each meal was filled with laughter. Henry, as the head of this family, made certain each child received praise and a hug each day. He instituted a prayer time each evening before bed, whispering to Annabella that his nanny had done that every evening. Nanny?

The four older children were becoming worthy horsemen. They each seemed to have a talent that was needed at the ranch. Molly had a skill handling all the animals, Patrick was growing into a strong young man and offered the muscle that sometimes seemed lacking in Charlie and Manuel; Toby and Skeeter were nimble as monkeys and able to make the work vanish.

And at least two evenings a week Dell and Will came by after dinner. The kids loved seeing Will, and Dell always managed to drift away for a private talk with Annabella.

On one of his visits Dell got a chuckle out of the new cabin decorations. It appeared that Annabella had made curtains for all the windows of the cabin from the fabric of the traveling dress she had been wearing on her arrival at the ranch. Since that day Dell had not seen her in another dress. She liked her cowpoke clothing. On those visits he would look at her and wonder if her heart was still guarded - especially those times that she greeted him with a welcoming smile.

CHAPTER 10

One day late in the summer an Indian rode up to the house. Skeeter was beside himself. He had been waiting for the wild west to come calling and it finally did. The man ignored everyone at the ranch and went directly to Morning Flower. They spoke for some time and then she pulled Henry into the conversation. It was a very serious discussion.

Finally Henry came to Annabella. "Running Elk wants some help."

"Who is he?" she asked.

"He's the squaw's grandson. He and the rest of the tribe live in the hills."

"I thought the government had moved the Indians to special lands."

"Not all them Indians think that's a good idea. Running Elk and his tribe stay away from government folks."

"But they talk to you."

"We sort of work together," was Henry's cryptic reply.

Now Annabella was curious. "What kind of help does he need?"

Henry hung his head. "It's hard to explain to a nice lady like you. I would help him, but now that you and the young'uns are here, I don't know." Annabella waited. Finally, "His wife, Willow, was raped by some fellow from the Double B. He knows he can't report it or kill the man, but she needs some care and so do his two children. The rest of the tribe wants to leave and let Running Elk and his family fend for themselves."

Annabella gasped. "I thought the tribe worked for everyone."

"I think they're worried Running Elk will do something to strike back and put their small band at risk."

"Will you take them in?" Annabella was already calculating space and food.

"That's what I'm asking you," said Henry. "Can they come here and will you and the children feel safe?" Since Annabella's arrival Henry had treated her as a valued advisor. He included her in discussions with Manuel and Charlie about planning work, designing the cabin addition and shopping trips to town. She had eased smoothly into the role and often added value to every discussion as well as a clear plan for implementation.

"How old are the children?"

"About Missy's and Byron's age."

Annabella smiled. "Two more children for my school. What will his wife need?"

xxx

Running Elk returned late in the afternoon. Two small children rode atop his horse and the animal towed a strange contraption made of skins and poles. His wife was bundled in the furs. The two children were wide-eyed and solemn. Running Elk led the horse with a quiet dignity. Annabella was touched by his protection toward his family and awed by the elegance in his bearing.

Six children came running to see this unusual sight. Spying the woman bundled behind the horse caused them to stop and stare. Morning Flower rushed to the family and Annabella joined her. Running Elk spoke in his tribal language. Morning Flower responded in kind. She turned to Annabella. "He fears that her arm is broken."

Annabella quickly assessed the situation and began issuing orders to the children. "Patrick help those babies off the horse. Molly, take them inside for a snack. Some bread and milk will do. I want you boys to help Running Elk lift this contraption and carry his wife into my room."

Morning Flower protested. "No."

"Nonsense," replied Annabella as she shooed Missy and Byron into the house with the Indian children. "Into my room," she told Patrick as he and the other boys grabbed on. Running Elk listened to Morning Flower and understood what was happening. He gestured to the boys and they carefully lifted his wife. Morning Flower scurried ahead while Annabella walked beside Skeeter, the smallest boy, just in case.

The small bedroom had slowly evolved over the last month into a quiet, clean, very feminine room. The big bed had matching blankets and curtains made of Annabella's clothing. There was a small table with a wash basin and several wash clothes and towels. Missy and Molly were learning how to be young ladies under Annabella's training. She shared with them her fragrant soaps and a lotion as they prepared for bed every evening. For the time being they would all move up to the loft with the boys.

Running Elk lowered his wife onto the bed as indicated. He and Morning Flower untied the bindings and slowly turned her onto the bed. Annabella came into the room with a basin of warm water. "Do you understand me?" she asked the Indian. He nodded. "Your grandmother and I will clean her and check her arm. You sit with your children." He nodded.

All of the children were gathered at the table watching the drama unfold. Molly had seen to feeding the small children. When Running Elk joined them, Skeeter asked, "Are you a real Indian? Did you hunt buffalo?"

"That's a dumb question," said Patrick. "There's no buffalo here."

Running Elk snorted. He stared at the six white children, mesmerized by Molly's strawberry blond and Patrick's carrot red hair. His children sat like little statues. He nodded to them and they reached for the bread and milk Molly had set on the table.

"We live mountains," he said in halting English. "We hunt rabbit and deer."

"Wow," replied Skeeter in an awestruck slow whisper. "You live in tents?"

"We like caves. Keep warm." They heard a cry come from the store room.

Annabella was grateful that Morning Flower had some skill with broken bones and other health treatments. The squaw had quickly and efficiently set Willow's arm. Next, the two women worked together to secure the arm and to make Willow comfortable.

The next step in Willow's care required the preparation of medicinals. Morning Flower ground some bark and mixed in seeds. She put the mixture in a cup and added boiling water. She took the cup to Willow as Annabella followed.

The two Indian women had a quick discussion. Morning Flower turned to Annabella. "No baby." Annabella gasped as she understood that Willow was drinking a potion that would prevent a pregnancy resulting from this attack. They then tended to her other bruises.

xxx

That evening Dell and Will came because they had heard about Willow. "How did you hear?" Annabella was always surprised at the speed of gossip along the plateau. Dell had shrugged. He had heard because his ranch hands reported that the Double B hand had bragged when he met the others clearing a fallen tree.

"Can you help me understand why this happened? Are the girls and I in danger?" Annabella scanned the horizon expecting attacking hordes to descend upon the ranch.

"You have to always be careful out here," advised Dell, wishing it were otherwise. "Some men are just mean. But, they first target the Indian women. Willow got caught too far away from the tribe. She didn't fight hard because her boys were close by hiding in the high grass."

"Didn't fight hard? She has a broken arm."

"Some men just think the woman needs to be beaten, too."

Annabella's stomach rolled. She gripped Dell's sleeve. "My girls."

Dell was worried about her. She had turned so pale. "We just have to make certain the boys understand to protect them and that the girls understand how to stay safe. Most of the troublemakers work at the Double B. We'll all keep an eye out for them coming to Henry's."

They talked in more detail about teaching the youngsters. Annabella knew that the plateau held the same dangers for women as Cincinnati, or anywhere else. Women had to always be aware of their own safety. To some men, a woman on her own was an invitation to assault. She looked across the pastures. At least on the ranch a woman should be able to see the danger coming and prepare.

With statehood women would get to vote. Annabella wondered if that meant men would treat women better. She doubted that getting the vote would change either men or women.

CHAPTER 11

Life had been lonely and sad for all the years Morning Flower had lived with Henry. But inviting those children had brightened her life. She adored each one, especially the two girls. But she always had to smile when she thought about little Byron. He was so young and probably didn't even have a memory of his mother. Not like Morning Flower, she had memories. Happy ones and devastating ones. She kneaded the bread dough letting her anger drive her hands.

"Morning Flower," Annabella spoke interrupting the vigorous assault on the dough. "Is something wrong?"

Morning Flower took her hands out of the dough and stood with her back to Annabella. "I . . ."

"I think you're lost in unhappy memories," said Annabella. The same kind of memories that sometimes haunt me, she thought. "Can I help you with something?"

The squaw turned and faced the new woman that had joined her household. "I worry you will send me off."

Annabella gasped. "Why would I do that?"

"I piece of furniture. And now family cause trouble."

"You're what? You're not making sense. And your family needs help."

"Henry own me. He trade for flour." She seemed to find an inner strength and stood tall. "I work hard but no wife, I be like cattle."

"Dell said that Henry bought you," said Annabella as she leaned against the wall. "Is that what happened?" It had been her experience that a relaxed pose often encouraged her students to talk about their misdeeds without feeling threatened.

Morning Flower sat in a chair and picked dough off her fingers. Annabella took over the dough and got it ready to be set aside to rise. "How did you get here?" she asked.

"I not remember."

Annabella gave her a challenging look.

"My tribe abandon me, left me to die." Annabella gasped. "We leave government land. We listen to leader who say we should run away and go back to old ways. Many follow him. We travel. We walk, we find no food. Some become weak. I have husband and son and my son have son."

"Running Elk?"

She nodded.

"What happened?"

"I get weak, no food, must walk, no ponies for everyone. Leader says I must be left behind to die. My husband and son follow like dogs. They leave me on trail. Running Elk young boy, but he try to stay with me. His father angry. I tell him to go. He return that night and bring me some food and water. Next day tribe goes further into mountains, but he comes back that night, more food. Then I not see him again. I rest on trail for days and grow weaker. I wake up in Henry's house."

"She was almost dead," said Henry. They hadn't heard him enter the house. "I found her on the trail and brought her back to the cabin. Me and Charlie took care of her. It took weeks, but she finally was strong enough to get out of bed and she began to cook for us. But she couldn't speak our language. Dell's pop could speak her tongue so he came over and talked with her. We all came to an understanding." Here Henry blushed.

Annabella waited for an explanation of the understanding. Henry wasn't eager to reply. Finally Morning Flower said, "I become Henry's squaw. I cook. He give me protection. We grow old together."

"How did you learn the language?" asked the teacher.

"Not easy. Dell and Will, young boys, they want to learn my talk - we share."

Annabella smiled. "You and the boys learned together?" Morning Flower nodded. Dell must know more of Morning Flower's language than he admitted.

"We was doing fine until the tribe leaders came back to get her," said Henry. "They said her husband was captured and jailed and one of the other men wanted her. I couldn't give her back to that tribe. They treated her so mean. So I said I would offer supplies in trade." He gave Annabella a sly smile. "They were hungry and happy to barter for food. We never saw them again."

Morning Flower nodded. "No one come to see. But old leader die and tribe wander, some go to homeland. Running Elk join with Willow. She not want to leave parents alone in the caves. Now not many remain. He come to me and ask for food for her and his boys." She gave a gentle smile to Henry. "He invite Running Elk to live here. Willow want to stay with mother and father. But they always need food."

"Running Elk is staying now," Annabella pointed out.

Henry spit in disgust. "When Willow was attacked her father didn't help her. Running Elk was out hunting. Willow was sorely pissed. She finally allowed Running Elk to seek help from us."

"Her father didn't help her?" Annabella was puzzled. "He let the man get away?"

Morning Flower had a fury in her eyes. "He say must protect tribe. Willow must suffer for tribe to be safe."

"What?" Annabella clutched the edge of the table to contain her anger.

Henry said, "Let me explain. The tribe knew that if they retaliated, the tribe would suffer for attacking white folks. But Morning Flower suspects that they set up Willow as sort of a trade for supplies."

"What?" Annabella was outraged. This just got worse and worse. "Her father?"

Henry nodded while he hugged Morning Flower as she tried to control her tears. "That's how the tribes survive, trading women for food. In my case, they left Morning Flower alone once I gave them provisions. In Willow's case, they would have bartered her favors until someone killed her. She is young and comely."

Annabella gave Henry a look that explained what she thought of men - all men. She pushed him aside and hugged Morning Flower. "Are the other women in the tribe safe from exploitation?"

"Willow is only squaw that attract men. The others are old or too skinny and dirty."

"When Running Elk returned what happened?"

Henry shrugged. "He won't tell us. But we think he wanted to fight the leader. He and his family were banished from the tribe. The leader can't stand for that sort of defiance or he loses control." Henry looked around the cabin to make certain no one else was listening. "We hear that leader has disappeared. They want Running Elk to return to lead and he told them all to go to hell." Henry grinned. "He could keep them healthy and protected. But he says he's done with them and wants his family to stay with us."

"What will happen to the rest of the tribe in the caves?"

Henry and Morning Flower both shrugged. Then Henry said, "They'll either come to one of the ranches for help or die. This winter is going to be harder than usual. I can feel it. And I can see it in the migratin' birds."

Again, Annabella thought that Henry was far better educated than he let folks know. She would wait to hear more of his story. "Will they seek help here?"

Morning Flower nodded. "Only women and children now, few men. They can't feed everyone. We wait and see. Running Elk brings food to them often."

"Even though he and his family were treated meanly."

"Many tribe members family," said the squaw. "We help."

Annabella understood.

xxx

Willow, Running Elk's wife, spent three weeks in bed, her arm had been set and she was healing, but she developed a fever and was in and out of consciousness during that time. In the beginning Annabella spent the night at her side and the two girls and the Indian children slept in the loft. Running Elk slept in front of the fireplace in the big room, always within earshot of his wife. They all relied on Morning Flower's knowledge of Indian potions to control the fever and prevent infections in the wounds.

Annabella was relieved when Willow finally opened her eyes. The Indian woman spoke very little English but she seemed grateful for the attention and care she had received. Over the weeks she learned several words as she started to move about the house to help Morning Flower with inside chores. Once she was out of bed, her children seemed to come alive. They laughed and demonstrated that they had been learning to speak English all during this time.

xxx

Annabella explained to Dell during one of his visits, "In my experience as a teacher, I have seen youngsters arrive in a community from Europe and within weeks be able to communicate with their new friends." They were watching Missy and one of the Indian boys play a game and argue over the rules.

As she explained this phenomenon Dell smiled at her because she always smiled back. "I've been working on Spanish and some Indian talk for years," he confessed. "Nothing seems to take." Another smile. "Guess I'm too old."

"Dell Rutherford," Annabella teased, "I know you learned Indian talk from Morning Flower," recalling Morning Flower and Henry explaining how she learned to speak.

"Got me." He threw back his head and laughed. "Somebody talked."

She liked these late summer evenings talking with Dell about nothing and watching the children play or listen to Henry entertain them with fantastic stories. If he were to be believed, Henry had sailed around the world, knew how to speak fifteen languages, had fought in every war for

73

the last thousand years, and had meet every famous person since Adam and Eve. The children loved each tale.

"I've been watching those youngsters ride," Dell said. "Molly and Skeeter have skill. They ride bareback and sometimes don't even use leads."

"Is that good for the horse?" Annabella was still not at ease on a horse.

"Let's just say," he explained, "since they're still too small to saddle those big bays, bareback is pretty useful." A burst of laughter from those listening to Henry. Even Will was enthralled with the stories this evening. "How're those Indians working out?"

Annabella sighed. "I think they're discussing taking a portion of the bunkhouse as their sleeping space. Will showed Henry that they could partition off a space with a wall and make another door. Another option is to remodel Henry's tool shed. And you can see that Henry has started a foundation for the addition of my room to the cabin." She shrugged.

"So they're going to stay?"

"I don't get into their conversations. Henry has indicated that the rest of the tribe is staying in touch but wants them to stay away. Running Elk can't support his family single handed and Willow isn't up to that nomadic life anymore. She is still very frightened. And Running Elk wants his children schooled." She smiled at Dell again. "School starts next week and I'll have eight children and five or six adults."

"Adults?"

"Charlie and Manuel want to learn to read and cipher. I think Running Elk is interested and maybe the women. Henry can already read." She thought for a moment. "In fact, I think he is very well read. All those stories he tells are Greek classics that he sets in the wild west.

"Damn," grinned Dell. "Excuse me. You just surprised me." He was quiet for a time wondering about Henry and education. Dell and Will had received a basic education from their parents. Then for a time they had each been sent to St. Louis to live and study with his father's brother. In those years summer was spent at the ranch and winter was spent in the city, learning. The man had been a barrister with a network of colleagues willing to help the two young ranchers gain skills in law and basic finance.

"My husband was well-educated," said Annabella. "He even wrote some stories and poetry." She played with her hands in her lap. "He always seemed to be so lost managing the store. I wondered if he wouldn't have been better suited as a professor."

That made Dell wonder. "You like that kind of man?" He knew that poetry was a foreign language to him.

It had grown dark and everyone had drifted into the house for a quick snack before bed time. The two of them stayed alone under the stars. Annabella finally said, "He had a lot of good qualities." She took Dell's hand, startling both of them. "You both have many qualities in common - kindness, warmth, understanding. But you also have strength and courage. I've watched you handle the children, and you have skill in dealing with people."

When Annabella realized she had grasped Dell's hand, she pulled hers back to her lap deciding to ignore the exchange. She could find nothing else to say.

Dell, for his part, thought this was a signal that maybe, just maybe, she would not spurn any warm gesture on his part. He would take it slowly, like working a skittish animal. But maybe, just maybe, on his next visit he might take her hand.

CHAPTER 12

Today Henry talked with Annabella about the cabin addition he had proposed as her own room. Once Running Elk and his family had taken over her room it became a higher priority. This morning he said to her, "Dell is sending over a few of his boys. We're going to get serious about your room." He paused and then added. "I think the girls will have to move in with you."

"I thought you were thinking about moving the family to the bunkhouse or the tool shed."

Henry rubbed the back of his neck in thought. "That might happen in the future but for now," he looked at her sadly, "Running Elk and my squaw think Willow needs to be close to all of us."

She nodded. "I understand. The girls and I have no problem with sharing space. We will all appreciate giving the boys back their privacy."

Henry gave her a sly look. "And we can make that space big enough for your bathing tub." Once Annabella had found the tub in his shed, she and the girls, and sometimes Morning Flower, enjoyed a weekly bath. Even little Byron could be convinced to play in the water if there were enough bubbles. Annabella's plan was to convince the other boys to use it once bathing in the river got too cold.

Henry was eager to build the addition since Morning Flower had volunteered their bedroom as the alternate bathing room. Once a week he had to bed down in a room that smelled like flowers. It was a smell that made him recall all that he had lost. Those years of his youth in Georgia, fragrant summers, a loving wife and a nurturing family of wealth and privilege. Those were bittersweet evenings as he recalled memories that he was certain were coaxed into his head by the lingering fragrance of Annabella's soaps. They were comforting, yet sad, reminiscences of those bygone years. Some nights he cried.

xxx

It took the crew two weeks to make the room a reality. The girls were delighted to get back to Annabella's nightly tutorial on ladylike preparations. Molly brushed her hair one hundred times and helped Missy count her strokes. Both girls enjoyed the tiny drop of lotion Annabella shared that they rubbed into their hands. "It makes us smell sweet," observed Missy.

To which Annabella always answered, "You are sweet. You are both the sweetest cowpokes I know." That always got a giggle. And sometimes she added, "You can be ladylike even in your britches."

"Even when we smell like chickens and horses?" asked Molly.

"People will know you are a young lady by your behavior, your kindness and your intelligence," she raised her eyebrow, "not by how you smell." She hoped the girls were understanding her subtle lessons.

Her real challenge was to raise four young gentlemen. The older boys had a natural protectiveness toward their siblings. That was a start. She thought about all the men they met on the plateau and decided that she might point out traits in each that the boys should emulate.

This evening she snuggled into her new bed, delighted that Henry had made three separate bunks instead of one large bed. In her usual evening review of the day she began cataloguing traits that the boys should acquire. She soon realized that each man the boys knew had many good qualities to follow. They were all protective, respectful of one another and courteous of women. They worked hard and were eager to learn. She thought the boys could learn a joy of life from Will and Manuel, dignity and personal pride from Charlie and Henry. Running Elk was a fine example of a dedicated and dutiful husband and father. And Dell. She sighed. In her mind he had all those traits. He was Dell and she wondered if she was . . . if he was . . . a future? She quickly pushed that thought away. And as she usually did when her thoughts got too speculative, she yawned deeply and fell asleep.

CHAPTER 13

Molly and Skeeter were the two children with a skill to handle the horses. The others could ride and care for the animals, but those two seemed to communicate with all the livestock. Somehow they seemed to know before everyone else when an animal needed care. One day Charlie was working with a horse, trying to get the beast into a corral. Molly stopped to watch and Skeeter came up beside her. "He won't go in," she said.

"Why not?" Charlie was puzzled and frustrated.

"He doesn't like the other horse."

"What other horse?" Charlie only had one horse with him and the corral was empty.

"The horse that's watching from the trees," said Skeeter.

"What horse in the trees?"

"That horse that keeps coming near the corral." Both kids pointed. Charlie stared into the trees on the hillside. He finally spotted the stallion.

"I've never seen that horse," said Charlie. "I've heard about him. He runs wild up near the canyons and caves."

"He wants our lady horses," said Molly.

"How do you know?" Charlie gaped at her.

"You can hear him call them," she said.

"Yeah," Skeeter agreed. "This guy," he gestured toward the horse on Charlie's lead, "Tells them to stay. He tells them it will be cold in the winter in the canyons and the food is better here."

"They like him better, but the wild horse keeps calling," said Molly.

Running Elk came into the yard. He scanned the trees. "Wild Wind come for women."

"What?" asked Charlie, still trying to get the horse under control.

"Him." The Indian pointed to the stallion in the trees.

"You know him? He yours?"

"Mountain spirits own horse. Want to make herd. Need mares."

"Tell him to go find someone else's mares." Charlie was not happy with this discussion.

"Okay." He looked up as Skeeter and Molly ran toward the trees.

Running Elk laughed. "They tell Wild Wind. He listen to them."

Charlie mumbled to himself as his horse finally walked into the corral.

xxx

Dell liked to tease Annabella about citifying the ranch. Tonight he was marveling at the privy walk. That's what he called it as he said, "That's the fanciest privy walk I've ever seen." He nodded toward the pebbled walkway that wound toward the small shack. Annabella had planted flowers and small undergrowth plants from the forest along the path. And in front of the two doors, she had convinced Henry to fashion an arbor and she was training a cluster of honeysuckle to climb the posts. Yes, two doors!

Dell and Will had laughed at that but Annabella had argued, "There are fifteen people in our household. And sometimes the children can't wait."

Will had smirked. "Those boys just have to step behind the barn."

Annabella had scowled at him. "I am raising gentlemen not barbarians."

Dell had loved watching the exchange. Annabella was starting to show character. A new woman, one who let you know what she thought.

But he also liked to push. "Are you planning on adding indoor plumbing like the cities? I've seen installation plans and kits in that there Sears and Roebuck catalog." He smirked.

She gasped in delight. "You have? Maybe Henry would be agreeable since he's finished the cabin addition." She was thoughtful, then added, "And imagine running water in the kitchen." She smirked back. "We could be the first on the plateau with indoor water and things."

"Maybe Will and I would like a water closet at our place." He took her hand and led her to their bench. "It would make the house a great place to bring a wife."

"Are you looking for a wife?" She felt breathless.

"Are you looking for a husband?"

She shrugged. "I already have six children." She was silent and let him toy with her fingers. "Maybe they would like a father." She gave him a sidelong look. Was she flirting?

He looked at their hands. "Does that mean you might let me court you?" He had been thinking about this for several weeks and tonight seemed to be the right time to ask.

She withdrew her hand. "I have to think about that. What would it mean for the children and all these people?"

"Courting just lets us get to know us better." He pulled her to her feet. "Everything else will work out." He gave her a kiss on the cheek and escorted her back to the house.

Since he might be courting her, Dell decided to study the catalog later at home to see if he could bring plumbing into his old homestead. Women were trouble. He thought his father had mentioned that a time or two over the years.

XXX

That evening Annabella lay in bed thinking about courting and what Dell would mean to her life. She was content, possibly for the first time since her brother exiled her to St. Louis. Did she want another husband? She was already cooking and cleaning and caring for six children. What did marriage have to offer? Sex? It had not been important to her marriage, just something she never quite got the hang of.

Maybe there was something wrong with her. Maybe she should warn Dell that she was lacking in any marriage skill. She was best at teaching, not being a wife.

On the other hand, did she really look forward to being lonely for the rest of her life? Even though the house was filled with life and people, she felt as though she were in a cocoon. Life had not been as frightening for her as it had been for the children, or as hard scrabble as it had been for Henry and Charlie, or as filled with terror as it had been for Willow and Morning Flower.

Living in a cocoon had prevented her from developing emotions. That caused her to pause. Emotion? Did she have any? She didn't rage in anger, nor screech in delight, nor sob uncontrollably at life's challenges. If she had no emotions that must mean she had no passion - that emotion that danced through the novels she read. Maybe that was why sex with Mr. Winters had had no luster.

That's it, she thought. No passion! If she were correct, she had no skill for marriage, she had no passion. Did one have passion, or did it happen? Now she was being silly, she told herself. She was who she was, a good teacher and a lonely, reserved woman. Holding hands with Dell in the moonlight didn't change anything.

She had a lot to think about tonight and promptly fell asleep.

CHAPTER 14

When September came Annabella started her school as promised. In the morning the children did chores then settled in the great room for lessons once breakfast had been cleared. After lunch the older children were released to work while Willow's two small boys, Byron and Missy stayed with Annabella to get some more intense schooling.

After dinner, Annabella ran her adult school. And found that the four older children who already knew reading and math basics were willing to act as tutors for the adults. Henry proved to be a valuable assistant teacher. He had a hidden cache of literature books and delighted in sharing the stories. He encouraged the children to read aloud.

By nine every evening, all the students stumbled to bed with a last snack of buttered bread and warm milk. Annabella told them all, adults and children, that they would remember their lessons better on a full stomach.

Once school started Dell found that his evening visits were only welcome on Saturday and Sunday. All the other days were dedicated to studies. If he did visit during the week, he always got drawn into conversations about the Iliad or Roman history with Charlie or Henry or helping Manuel and Morning Flower with cyphers. Sometimes he allowed the boys to complain about studying so much. He figured it was a way for them to let off steam.

He found he enjoyed tutoring. Charlie and Manuel were very eager to learn. Morning Flower needed a lot more help because she came from a culture without letters and numbers that resembled American letters and numbers. The squaw was so joyful when she finally mastered the alphabet and could recognize and write each letter.

By October, Annabella realized that she had to shorten her school hours. There was a lot to do on the ranch to prepare for winter. The older children were needed for ranch work. School was now a three morning and three evening event with the understanding that once the snows arrived, classes would resume full time. The children groaned at that announcement.

Life went on. Everyone studied and worked. And Dell kept visiting.

xxx

The autumn had arrived on the plateau. The children were moaning about school starting. And Dell was enjoying time with Annabella this quiet evening. Once he had indicated that he was interested in courting her, he had made a point of arriving at the ranch whenever possible after dinner, sometimes with Will and sometimes alone. He always took her hand and led her to a seat behind Morning Flower's garden.

Always helpful, Henry had added a low stone wall and trellis, screening Annabella's garden bench. He had whispered to Dell that it was a spot with a view of the sunset and what Dell made of it was up to him. Dell had smiled at the interest and support he was receiving. Will had also made certain to offer Dell some pointers. "I know you don't get into town to see the ladies much," Will had observed several weeks ago, "So I'll help out any way I can. Do you have any questions?" Dell had knocked him off his horse. "Is that a no?" Will had asked as he dusted himself off. "You're getting old and might have forgotten a few things."

"I haven't forgotten anything," Dell had growled, "except the next time I visit Annabella I'm going to forget to tell you."

Tonight was a clear cool evening. "What a pretty sunset this evening," said Annabella just as Dell said, "We need rain," preoccupied with its lack.

"Is it critical?" she asked, not familiar with the importance of weather. In the cities, it came and went, and life carried on.

"Another week and the fields will be too dry and at risk of fire."

"Fire?"

Dell took her hand. They had a routine. They sat, he held her hand and the conversation often had nothing to do with courting. "If a fire flares up," he began, "have the youngsters ride the horses up to a cave and leave those cows. There's not much to burn there. Make certain they stay away from the stand of trees." He liked the feel of her hand and hoped one day to feel more of her. "In fact, we should make plans with Running Elk to scout out a cave." Dell thought about this embryo plan for fire protection. "Let me think some more. Tomorrow I'll come by and I'll talk to Henry and get an evacuation plan ready."

"You're serious," she gasped. "I had no idea that fire was a danger."

"All that acreage we and Henry have in grass is for winter for the stock. If it gets dry, it's easy to harvest. If it gets too dry it may burn. Couple more weeks of no rain, we have to worry."

"Is that acreage yours or Henry's?" she asked. "He doesn't seem to have a lot of livestock."

Dell squeezed her hand. "You have a good eye. Henry grows it for our ranch. He stores it and I buy it as I need it. It's a good income for him and I don't need to build bigger storage." A night bird cried and they stopped to listen.

She enjoyed these evenings, no matter the conversation. She was content to sit in the silence and gaze at the stars. But Dell had more to say this evening. "Part of courting," he tried to sound like a man of experience, "is to talk about marriage and a future together."

She sighed. She was finally allowing herself to sigh openly. She stared at their clasped hands. "I don't know what to tell you. I worry that I'm not the type of woman who will make you happy. I've been married and I found my wifely duties uninspired."

"Do you mean the bedding?" Dell would die before he would utter the word 'sex' in front of a lady.

"Yes," she said, still holding his hand, "Mr. Winters had requested that it be a part of the bargain." More silence. "I never seemed to be -

"Did he hurt you?"

"No, he was very much like his father, kind, gentle, and he appreciated my efforts. At least he mentioned that I was -

This was a difficult conversation for her. She blurted out. "I have no passion. I never longed for his touching like the novels say. I never found it necessary to sleep against his warmth. I was very content to sleep without being embraced." Since she had no concept of a marital bed other than her limited experience with Mr. Winters and dime novels, she was at a loss for words on the subject.

Dell, somewhat experienced with a saloon worker or two and in recent years an older widow, didn't understand the mystique of a marriage bed for women. He said, "I want a partner, someone responsible for running my household. I need you for your strength and intelligence, and your skill with those youngsters and the Indians and the cowpokes. You have a kindness and respect for everyone. That's real important out here where we rely on our neighbors."

"No bedding?"

Dell knew he was on shaky ground. He wanted to shout, "Hell, yes!" But he didn't want to scare her. Pausing to give it some thought he said, "We can always give it a try and we can decide if we want it to be a habit." He sent up a silent prayer that Annabella would see the light.

She accepted that explanation, thinking that maybe Dell felt as she did. "What about other children?"

"That's a good question," he replied. "I'd like us all to be a family with those we already have. Since you were bedded and have no children of your own, maybe you're barren."

She gasped in what sounded like a sob, all her old loneliness and sorrow and abandonment came together in that sound. Barren? Why did it matter? Now she was confused about her lack of interest in a marriage bed.

"Now don't be hurt," Dell tried to comfort her. "Look around, we have plenty of offspring to love."

To love? Annabella was struck by his statement. He wanted family and he wanted to love. Maybe it would be good to marry this thoughtful and serious man. The children would prosper and grow. She would be with someone who would be a protector and good provider. She'd have to think about the love part.

"I would like to form a strong family with the children. You would be a good father."

"Thank you." More silence. "If you're of a mind, we can think about a wedding at Christmas. The land will be resting. My responsibilities are less at that time."

"What about Henry?" she asked.

Dell was thoughtful, she sounded like she might like a reason to delay. He knew she was skittish and he shouldn't push. "Why don't we go along for a time to see if we agree? No one needs to know our thinking." Annabella relaxed. She acted as though the hangman gave her a reprieve. Dell knew he had made the right suggestion.

They rose from their bench and he kissed her cheek as he did every evening. As they returned to the cabin large raindrops began to fall, slowly at first and then the sky seemed to open up.

Dell and Annabella dashed through the kitchen door, laughing and brushing rain drops aside. "I guess I don't have to rush about making a fire plan," he said, "But we should take the kids up into the hills to see the caves and work on your riding skills."

CHAPTER 15

Annabella was becoming a reasonable horsewoman and the older children were riding as skillfully as old cowhands. On a sunny Sunday afternoon Dell, Will and Running Elk organized a trail ride into the hills. Running Elk hadn't contacted his tribe for several weeks and Morning Flower had packed some supplies for him to take to them.

Dell rode at the back watching for stray children. The first time Byron had been on a horse, riding behind his brother, he had slid off the horse's rear. It was decided that Byron had to ride with Will until he was older. But the young fellow seemed to enjoy his place in front of Will holding fast to the pummel or the horse's mane.

Missy liked riding behind her brother, Patrick. She held tight to his belt usually chattering the entire journey about the landscape or food or a story she had read in one of Miss Annabella's books.

Molly, Skeeter and Toby were following Running Elk, managing their horses skillfully through the sharp climbs and dry creek beds. They listened to every word as Running Elk pointed out safe caves for shelter, clean water sources, and edible plants. He also pointed out blind canyons with a warning to avoid those areas, trying to get the children to understand the dangers of flash flooding and wild animal lairs.

Will pulled his horse close to Dell. "Do you think they'll remember all this talk?"

"It's good information," replied Dell. "Of course, he'll have to tell them fifty more times."

Annabella dropped back to ask, "Are we in a dangerous drought?"

Dell shrugged. "We could use more rain than we got last week. I told you about lightning fire dangers."

She nodded, then pulled her mount up hard as almost magically the trail party was surrounded by Indians. There appeared to be eight men on ponies. Running Elk spoke to them and they turned, inviting the party to follow.

They climbed higher and moved into one of the passages similar to those Running Elk had warned were blind canyons. Once through the tight opening they moved along a narrow trail leading them to an open field and a small pond that appeared to be a natural spring that the Indians had trapped for a water supply. There was a corral and what looked like a garden. But the children were fascinated with the dwellings. The Indians had taken advantage of the caves along the canyon walls using the openings high up the wall as dwelling space and the lower openings for storage or animal shelter.

"I thought your tribe moved from the area," said Will.

Running Elk said, "They prepare for winter. They say it be difficult."

"How do they know?" Skeeter asked. He was the youngster most interested in native lore.

"The old man," Running Elk pointed to a gray-haired man slumped against the canyon wall as though he were napping. "He know the wind. He talk to the birds. The snows will be hard."

Annabella listened and asked Dell, "Should we believe his predictions?"

"It's always good to listen," said Dell, "The old tribe leaders have a good sense of the coming weather." As they dismounted, several members of the tribe came to greet them, curious to meet new people and delighted to receive the supplies.

Annabella spotted one young pregnant woman. She approached the woman and spoke the few words of greeting that Morning Flower and Willow had taught her. Dell stood with her and helped interpret. "You say the words very well," he commented.

"You speak their language with ease. Didn't you tell me once that languages eluded you?" She teased him, enjoying their growing familiarity.

"I didn't want to brag about my skill." He smiled at her. "I can speak some to the Mexicans and to the Indians and even to pretty teachers who come calling." She blushed. He enjoyed it.

"When will this woman have her child?" Annabella asked him. "My language isn't that good."

He spoke to the woman and told Annabella, "She says she will have a child in three moons. I guess somewhere close to Christmas."

"Would it be rude or insulting, if I invited her to the cabin for her birthing?" Annabella looked at the stark surroundings and tried to imagine it during the harsh winter the old man was predicting.

"I can relay your invite," he said, "She will be flattered. I'll tell her you are speaking for Morning Flower." He spoke to the woman as the other women of the tribe gathered to listen. They nodded and smiled, then the pregnant woman replied. Dell translated, "She says to thank Morning Flower, but she feels comfortable here. One of these women is an experienced midwife." Annabella smiled at all the women and they smiled in return.

Will caused a stir when he unpacked his saddlebags and presented their hosts with additional foods from his ranch. Although the Indians invited the riders to stay for a meal, Running Elk was eager to return to the ranch before dark. He had left his family at Henry's ranch. The squaws sent back gifts for Willow and the boys. After an exciting visit the men led them back out of the canyon and onto the trail that would take them home.

As they came out of the maze of trails to the ridge line, they were able to see Henry's ranch in the distance. "They can watch us like angels in heaven," said Molly as she watched the Indians take positions on the bluff.

Annabella smiled at the thought as she followed Molly and the others down the trail and back to the ranch.

CHAPTER 16

There was always so much to do. At least once a month Annabella found she had to go into town with one or two children for new shoes, new clothes - who knew children grew this fast. And soon she would have to talk with Molly about growing into a young woman. She could see the signs. She was glad she had taken Dell's advice and dressed the girls in trousers. It was one protection against the dangers to young women in the wilderness. She laughed to herself as she thrust her legs out. She had adopted trousers, too, and enjoyed the freedom. She never worried when she had to scurry up the ladder to the boys' sleeping loft. She didn't panic when Henry told her it was time for a riding lesson. And she certainly didn't worry when she had to get down on her knees to pull weeds. These rancher trousers were sturdy.

She yawned into the silence and thought about her concerns during the first days on the ranch. They seemed to have evaporated. The children were happy, lively and content. Henry, Morning Flower and the two ranch hands were doting grandparents. This was turning into something she had never imagined.

Then she wondered. Was she becoming a different Annabella? Or was she finding the old Annabella? She wasn't certain. She still kept her emotions contained, but she knew the children were taking over her heart.

xxx

It was another night under the stars. Dell and Annabella's courting ritual was supported by the entire family. They always found time alone and to Dell's surprise always found something to talk about. He knew her story. His heart broke when he thought about the way she had been sent off from her roots. And he blessed his parents for the firm family life in which they had cocooned him and Will.

It had become his practice, his pleasure, to take her hand. One evening he said, "You can feel the season changing. It always starts with the evenings cooling." He took her hand and caressed it in his. "I can feel your fingers taking a chill. I'll keep them warm for you." She hadn't looked at him, but he was delighted when he felt her fingers relax in his grasp.

This was a bold step for Dell. He had always been a quiet, reserved man. His intermittent relationship with that widow in Deep Wells was all her idea. In fact, she had told him that she had needs and he was a safe man. His mind drifted recalling their exchanges. Always satisfying for him and pleasant. He wasn't certain what she thought. She always smiled as she saw him out the door with a quick kiss on the cheek.

"You're woolgathering," Annabella said with a smile. "I thought I was the one always guilty of that."

He gave her hand a gentle squeeze. "These quiet nights make a man think."

"I hope they are pleasant thoughts."

Dell could feel himself blush and was glad the evening was dark. "I like to reflect on the life I've been blessed to lead."

Annabella patted his hand. "You've never told me your story, Dell. How did the Rutherfords get to the plateau?"

He was grateful that she wanted that story and not to explore his thoughts at the moment. "The government divided this land after the war and after the Indians in these parts were resettled. There had been some big battles leaving troops and tribes both diminished. This was land the government wanted to give as a reward to soldiers and help spread settlers. We all moved in about the same time. Several men quickly sold their land and moved on. Ranching is hard work. My pop had some savings and was able to buy out folks. The other ranchers still here did the same. We finally became Henry, our ranch, Double B, Bar Eight, and Double X. Our ranch is the biggest and most prosperous. Double B is the worst run. When his daddy died, Billy at Double B hadn't learned how to run a ranch. The others worked hard and learned from each other. Except for Henry, we're all the next generation. Bar Eight and Double X are two generation households. The sons have their parents still living with them." He caressed her hand as he spoke. "I guess we're the same story as everyone else. Some prosper, some grow and some fail. And we keep working hard." He was quiet again as he thought about what to say. Finally, "I think about our future here a lot. The other ranches aren't as prosperous. Someday Will and I would like to buy them out if they want to move on. Double B won't leave. He's got no place to go and he'd have to use the money from the sale to pay debts and mortgages and things. No real gain for him." He pointed over her shoulder. "There's another plateau over that ridge with a few more of the original land grant farms. I think some of those may go for sale in a few years, too."

Annabella looked into the darkness. "Isn't that too far from your ranch?"

"There's a trail over the ridge. You can't move cattle over it, but it makes the land close enough to manage." He rubbed her hand and thought. "That's the future I see, Annabella. Expanding, having land for me and Will and our families." They heard Molly giggle. "A place for all our children."

"That's the future, Dell. But how did it begin? Your parents made certain you were well educated," she observed. "You speak well. You are good with cyphers."

"Our mother was educated and our pop had been a cavalry officer. In the winter they taught us. When I was old enough, they sent me to live with my father's brother in St. Louis for several winters for higher schooling. I read law with my uncle."

"You're a lawyer?" She couldn't hide the shock in her voice.

"Are you surprised I studied so much?" He brought her hand to his lips in a spontaneous move.

"No." She laughed softly, feeling herself blush at his affection. "I'm surprised you chose ranching over lawyering." She was silent a moment. "No, I'm not surprised. You seem so content with the life you lead. Your ranch, your work and your brother are important to you." She thought for a moment. "What about Will? Did he study, too?"

Dell laughed. "Will enjoyed his winters away from the ranch. He studied and had fun. He read law, too. We both decided that big cities and closed space were not for us. Our uncle was a wealthy man and left us some money. He died after our parents, and the money he left will allow us to buy more land and hire more ranch hands and improve things when the time is right."

"You and Will have been blessed. You have each other and a life that you can share."

Dell took a deep breath. "Will and I know what we have. And we know what we don't have. We don't have the life Mom and Pop had together." He looked at her in the dark night, her face in shadow. "It's the life I hope to find with you and all those kids."

He heard a small gasp. She seemed to be breathless. Finally, she acknowledged him, squeezing his fingers and saying. "It will be an honor for me to make that life together with you."

xxx

"Dell," Annabella had been thinking about something for the last few evenings. He could tell. She was finally ready to put it into words. "When were you in St. Louis? I taught school there for three years."

He rumpled his hair as he thought, gave her the years. "I was only there from November to March. I couldn't be spared for the whole year."

"We may have overlapped one year. What if we had met then?"

He laughed. "I was too shy and my uncle kept me close to his place. When Will schooled with him, he was more lenient. Or Will was sneakier. We didn't do social things. We hunted and went to his gentlemen's club for cards. He introduced me to some cousins over the years. But I never stayed in touch when I returned to the ranch."

"Why not? Family seems important to you."

He nodded. "To me yes, not to them. I think they wanted Uncle's money. With us out of the picture they thought they would get it." He rubbed a finger along her knuckle. "When he died he gave them his house and gave me and Will the cash. They didn't know that he came to the ranch several times over the years. They thought he had forgotten us."

"Do you keep up with them now?"

"No, I think they like it that way."

She sighed and snuggled against his shoulder. "Sometimes I wonder about my brother. He was my only family. But over the years he has never returned my letters. When I moved to a new town to marry Mr. Winters, I never wrote to him again. I wonder if he thinks of me?"

"Probably not." She gasped but he continued. "He thinks he treated you fairly when he gave you your inheritance share. The two of you probably led different lives growing up." She nodded. "He doesn't know what he cut from his life."

"How sad for me and for him." She snuggled closer. Dell wondered if she realized her movements.

"We'll teach our children to stay together and to help one another." He sat very still, tempted to put an arm around her. But he worried he would frighten her.

"And not to send their sisters away." She put her cheek on his shoulder.

"Amen." He smiled to himself.

xxx

Annabella rested on her bed. Dell had, as usual, spent time with her on the garden bench this evening. She thought about that and thought some more. She had so little experience with men that she wasn't certain if this was a budding friendship or just a response to the lack of interacting with any other adult of a certain age. She did what she always did, searched herself for her feelings. Were there feelings? Would she know feelings? Were they appropriate? And what feelings were appropriate -

friendship or something deeper? She had been married and knew that sex in her marriage had been nothing like the novels she read.

Was Dell one of those men that women were warned about - exploitive and threatening? She thought long about that possibility. And came to a conclusion. No, he wasn't! She knew him well. He was kind and interesting and he cared about the children. In fact, she had to smile at the fathering he lavished on his brother, Will. Dell took his role as big brother seriously.

That thought led to thoughts of her brother. He might not answer her letters, but she wanted him to know that she was still alive. She listened to the girls deeply asleep in their bunks. Annabella wanted him to know that she was happy that she had found life, that elusive excitement that made her want to share. She would write to him one more time. Maybe this time he would write in return.

She stared at the ceiling thinking of her brother and of Dell. As usual, as her thoughts became complex, she promptly fell asleep.

xxx

One day a rancher came by and shouted for Henry. "Hey, old man. I thought you should have this one." He pulled a yellow puppy out of his jacket. "No question who his daddy is." The puppy looked like a miniature of the chicken watch dog. "I told you he got to my bitch." The man laughed.

Henry stared at the puppy squirming in the rancher's hands. "Doggy," squealed Byron. He stepped to the man on horseback and held out his arms. The rancher laughed again.

"Someone agrees with me."

Henry looked at Byron and couldn't resist. "I guess he belongs with his daddy." He took the pup and handed it to Byron who seemed to levitate in delight. The youngster and the pup ran off as the rancher and Henry got down to other business.

For days everyone watched Byron carry the puppy everywhere. "He has legs," became the daily comment from everyone.

"He can't sleep in your bunk," was Annabella's daily comment. Until finally she said, "Byron, he can sleep with you when he knows how to do his business outside."

"Bidness?"

"When he poops and pees outside," explained Skeeter. "We don't want to step into a pile of -" He stopped speaking and looked around for Annabella who had become distracted by one of the other kids. Then finished, "Shit."

"Shit," said Byron.

And Annabella appeared. Skeeter didn't know how she did that. "What did you say?" She glowered at Byron. "I've told you before that is not a nice word."

The little boy did what he always did. He ran to her and clasped her leg, smiling up with his angelic expression. And it worked. She pulled him into her arms and gave him a kiss on the cheek.

Skeeter was disgusted. "He wants that puppy to poop in our bed." How did Byron get away with everything?

Annabella gave him one more hug, then put him back down. "Byron, your puppy has to learn to do his puppy business outside before he can sleep with you."

"Bidness?"

"I told you," Skeeter growled, clearly at his wits' end. "Poop and pee outside, not in our beds."

Annabella knelt before the boy. "Do you understand what Skeeter is saying? Your puppy can't sleep with you until he," she didn't know how to delicately say it.

"Until he pees and poops outside," said Henry in his this-is-my-law voice. "Understand?"

Byron nodded. He picked up the puppy and carried him to the plantings by the privy. From the cabin they watched as he talked and gestured to the small animal. Everyone laughed.

xxx

Even as winter and cold weather approached Dell continued to arrive in the evening for talk on the garden bench. I wonder if Henry has noticed, Annabella wondered. Morning Flower had made a comment. The kids were probably oblivious. But Will seemed to enjoy making remarks to Dell that no one but she and Dell could hear and Dell always glowered at him. They had still not told anyone that they had agreed to marry.

Annabella smiled to herself. Then almost bolted upright in her narrow bed. She smiled? While thinking of Dell? She searched herself as she realized she seemed to be doing more and more smiling. Where her defenses crumbling? Was she encouraging Dell? Did she want to encourage him? Was she reading more into his attention than he intended?

xxx

When she first started accompanying Henry into town, Annabella had found the local women aloof. They didn't know what to think of a woman who wore trousers and a broad brimmed hat just like the men who worked on the ranches. She even adopted the footwear, choosing a comfortable boot that she wore as she worked her garden or practiced her horsemanship.

But she was finally old news and on this visit the minister's wife stopped to speak. She was accompanied by her lovely daughter. Annabella seemed to remember some talk at the farm about the young woman and Will exploring a relationship. Henry called a greeting to the women as he stopped the wagon at the general store.

"Mrs. Blantry, and Miss Blantry," he always used his Southern charm with women. He smiled, tipped his hat and bowed slightly as he jumped down and met the women on the boardwalk in front of the store. "You two ladies brighten a fellow's day."

"Mr. Winters, you are a sweet talker." Mrs. Blantry even giggled.

Henry smiled and asked, "Have you had the opportunity to meet my daughter-in-law, Annabella Winters?" Both women gave her a small smile.

Young Miss Blantry spoke. "We are happy to meet you, Mrs. Winters. Please call me Margaret Ann." She grinned at Annabella, "But everyone calls mama Mrs. Blantry."

"Now, Margaret Ann, you shouldn't make Mrs. Winters think I put on airs."

"I understand," said Annabella, "You have a responsibility as the minister's wife to keep a dignified reserve."

"I like that," nodded Mrs. Blantry, "A dignified reserve." She gave Annabella a conspiratorial nudge. "I just don't like my given name. And I won't tell you what it is."

Annabella laughed. "A woman has to take a stand."

"Why don't you ladies visit while I pick up our supplies?" suggested Henry.

"But I must get some things for the children," said Annabella."

"Now, dear," said Mrs. Blantry, "Do your shopping and stop by our home for tea, while Henry does his business. We will be home within the hour." She pointed to a clapboard house sitting beside the small church. It was agreed and everyone proceeded with their tasks for the day.

Soon Annabella found herself sitting in a clean dining room looking at a china tea pot and lovely chinaware. It was a strange feeling; she had not been in such a civilized situation for months. She shifted uncomfortably in her farm wear. "Mrs. Blantry, you are too kind and I'm a horrible guest, dressed for farming and sitting in your lovely home."

"Don't worry, dear," said the minister's wife. "I think those trousers look very comfortable." She waited for a confirmation.

"They are," admitted Annabella. "I never thought of dressing this way, but Mr. Rutherford suggested that I dress the girls in trousers. He suggested that girls were safer if they didn't look like little girls when they live out on the range."

Margaret Ann gasped. "They would be harmed?"

Annabella shrugged. "He didn't go into detail. I just respected his recommendation. Then I decided that I could spend a lot of time making and mending dresses for me, but there is so much work to do on the ranch. Sewing isn't that important. I need time to tend my garden, keep house for the children, help Henry, teach."

"Teach?"

"Yes, I have been a teacher for many years. Each morning I teach the children, each evening I teach some of the ranch hands and Indians."

"Indians?" Margaret Ann seemed to be astounded by the commentary of Annabella's life.

"Yes," Annabella smiled. "Henry has given shelter to an older Indian woman and her family has moved in to also help work the ranch."

"You live with Indians. Aren't you afraid, if not for yourself, for the children?"

"Now Margaret Ann," her mother cautioned, "I'm sure Mrs. Winters keeps the savages at a distance."

"They aren't savages," corrected Annabella, "they are very polite and hardworking individuals. And they are very eager to learn."

"Well, of course they are," snipped Mrs. Blantry, "they see education as the way to better themselves and to try to rise above their station." She shook her head. "Lord knows they are not high on the list of God's children. They were heathens mere years ago. I surely don't trust that they have forgotten their pagan ways so quickly."

"I -," but Annabella got no further in her defense of Morning Flower's family.

"Oh, Mama," cried Margaret Ann, "I can't see myself moving to the ranch with Will. I could be killed or ravished in my bed."

"Daughter," Mrs. Blantry nodded, "I think you're right. You think twice about allowing that man to court you. I would worry day and night knowing you were living close to those heathens." Mrs. Blantry seemed to remember her guest. "Why, Mrs. Winters, I certainly hope that Mr. Winters has those heathens under control. For your sake and those innocent children."

"I -," again Annabella got no further.

"How many children did you take from the orphan train?"

"Six."

"Lord bless you," prayed Mrs. Blantry. "But I suppose that there is a lot of work on the ranch, and they give service for their keep. It doesn't do to let those sorts of youngsters get the better of you with their laziness and wasteful ways."

"The children all have chores. Of course, two of them are very young."

"It makes no mind. They have to understand how grateful they should be for your feeding them and such. Work will prepare them for when it's time for them to move on. You know once they turn to fifteen or so."

"Oh, Mama," smiled Margaret Ann, "you are generous. We know everyone in town turns out their orphans at twelve to apprentice or find paying jobs."

Annabella opened her mouth to challenge her hostess, but there was a knock at the door. It was Mr. Winters. Removing his hat as he entered the small house, he said, "Annabella, it's getting late and we want to get back before dark."

"Certainly, Henry." She gathered her packages and hat. "Thank you for the tea. But Henry is right. Everyone will worry if we're too late returning." She almost ran to the wagon.

Turning to wave at the women as they stood in the doorway, she heard Henry chortle. "They give you their opinion on Indians and orphans and things?"

"How did you know?" she gasped as she climbed on the wagon. "They were intolerable and intolerant. They think Morning Flower's family is planning to murder us in our beds. And they think little Byron should be working the fields. And I should send the children off to find paying jobs when they are twelve."

Henry laughed. "We'll be up on the plateau where the air is cleaner soon enough."

But Annabella frowned. "I think I ruined Will's romance with Margaret Ann."

"No, you didn't. Will already knew what you learned today. He couldn't see himself hitched to someone so tied up in white man's Christianity."

CHAPTER 17

Annabella's school was working well. She had just finished the morning lessons and the older children would have lunch and run out to help with chores. Henry had explained that there was a lot to do to get the ranch ready for winter. He stood by his prediction that winter would be harsh this year.

Lunch was over and she allowed the smaller children time to play before organizing them for their afternoon studies. Making this free time for her, a term that made her almost laugh. There was no free time on a ranch, she was using the time to complete a task not related to teaching or cooking or cleaning. She sat on the bunk in her new bedroom and looked through her remaining clothes, those reminders of those days when she wore dresses, stockings and delicate shoes.

She assessed her inventory. Talking with Dell about courting and maybe a wedding sometime in the future, she evaluated each remaining dress for its bride potential. After all she thought she should wear a dress to her own wedding. She was distracted by the thought of how easy sewing was since she had found that sewing apparatus in Henry's shed. She had made draperies, blouses for the girls, and investing in a red check flannel had made all the boys nightshirts. The red check remnants brightened the cabin, especially since she had also made small flannel cloths to be used as washcloths or napkins or handkerchiefs.

Dell teased her about being a red check menace. She had then presented him with his own red checked handkerchief. He had laughed and hugged her. Her heart had done a small flutter and she noticed he carried it with him.

Thinking of Dell brought her back to her task - a wedding dress. As a teacher she had a wardrobe of somber, serviceable clothing - nothing bright or flowery or wedding looking. As she thought about her dress, Molly charged into the room. "I lost my shirt button."

Annabella looked up as the youngster took off her shirt and hunted for another. She gave her old clothing to Annabella who said, "I have a button. This evening we'll have a sewing lesson."

Molly moaned. "The boys." Her old refrain when she wanted to point out that she was forced to learn skills not required of the boys.

Annabella thought about that. "You're correct. Everyone should learn to sew on buttons. That will be our lesson this evening." Then she was inspired. Over the weeks on the ranch she had noticed that Manuel tended very well to his clothing, always replacing buttons and patching garments when needed. She would ask him to help with the lesson. That might sideline the boys' complaints about women's work.

"Dresses," sighed Molly. She ran her fingers over a dress of a soft green fabric with a lace trimmed bodice. "I don't have any dresses."

"I only have these few left myself," admitted Annabella. She held the green dress up in front of Molly. The color complemented the youngster's fair coloring. "Maybe we each need a dress for special occasions. Do you think?"

Molly nodded in delight. "When?"

Annabella smiled at her enthusiasm. "The next time I go into town, I'll look at some of Mr. Purdy's ready-made dresses and at his fabrics. We'll have dresses for Christmas."

"And shoes?" asked Molly. "I can't wear a dress with these boots."

"And a hair ribbon?" Annabella asked.

"Oh, yes." Molly was lost in her imagination, a dress, shoes and ribbons. She finished buttoning her shirt. "I have to get back to the chickens." And she was gone.

Annabella threw back her head and laughed. She would have to tell this to Dell. He enjoyed the stories about daily life with the children.

xxx

"What did you say to Margaret Ann?" Will asked Annabella as he found her working in the kitchen garden, picking the last of the late vegetables and the herbs ready for drying that Morning Flower would use for her remedies and teas.

She stood and blushed. "I think I allowed her to misunderstand our lives here. She seemed to be worried that Morning Flower's family were planning to kill us." Annabella brushed dirt from her knees. "She also didn't seem to care about our children, or any orphans."

Will smiled at her. "You solved my problem. I've been staying away because I couldn't figure out how to withdraw my pledge."

"You planned to marry her?"

"No, I had just talked to her father about courting her. She kisses real sweet."

Annabella laughed. "I'm sure there are other young women in town." She reached up and ruffled his hair. "And you're such a handsome fellow."

"Don't tell him that," growled Dell as he joined them in the garden. "He'll spend all day tomorrow looking at his reflection in the river instead of watering the herd."

CHAPTER 18

Another busy day. Annabella had taught her morning classes and had just gotten the smaller children settled at their worktable to practice their letters when they heard shouting in the farm yard. Willow and Morning Flower rushed in from the garden with a panicked look in their eyes.

"Not good," muttered the older woman, "white men maybe want Running Elk."

"Why?" Annabella was pushing the children toward Willow's bedroom.

"No reason." The two Indian women moved through the cabin planning to race out the front door into the yard.

Annabella stopped them. "You two stay with the children. I'll send the others in to be with you." She dashed out into the yard.

". . . . and I want that water back," demanded the rumpled, bearded man astride a tired looking horse.

"I ain't done nothing to your water," shouted Henry. "Me and my hands got our own work to do. We don't have time to fiddle with your water."

"It ain't running like it used to. Somebody's stopping it." The stranger glowered at Henry. "I better get my water back or you'll pay."

"You got enough water," said Charlie as he and Manuel moved to stand with Henry. "That river is enough for all of us. The Rutherfords ain't complaining."

"The Rutherfords don't get any water from the north branch. That's just mine and yours." The cowboy spat. "So what are you doing to the flow? You blocking it or something? Taking more than your share?"

"We ain't done a thing to the north branch. We don't need it for much but watering my livestock." Henry stood his ground. Charlie and Manuel stood with him.

Annabella scanned the yard for the children. She finally found them peeking out of the barn loft. Patrick was keeping them quiet as they watched the drama. She also noticed several riders waiting at the crest of the hill at the far side of the hay field. They formed a line of silhouettes against the horizon. Annabella shivered. She walked into the yard to stand with Henry.

"Who's she?" demanded the cowboy.

"She's my daughter." Henry moved closer to her. "Now you get off my property. We ain't done nothing to the water."

"We'll see." The cowboy turned his horse. "I won't do nothing yet. I'll give you a chance to fix things. But if nothing happens. You'll pay." He was off, leaving them in the rising dust of his departure.

Annabella grasped Henry's arm. "Who was that?"

"Billy from the Double B." Henry spit on the imprints of Billy's horse. "He says we stopped up the north branch."

"North branch?"

Henry took off his hat and slammed it on his thigh. "His ranch and our ranch share the north branch. It flows from the hills through my place and on to his. It's smaller than the other, the south branch that goes through my place, and between Double B and Dell's place."

"What has him upset?"

"He thinks I'm blocking the water in the north branch." Henry turned to Charlie. "When you get some time go see what's happening to the water."

Charlie nodded. "I can probably go Saturday. We should have all the haying done by then."

Annabella looked off to the mountains. "How far away is the source of the water?"

"I don't know," replied Charlie, "I never looked for it before now. It was just always running."

Annabella's eyes ached trying to trace an invisible line of water into the mountains. "Why does he think you did something?"

"Because he's an ass," grumbled Henry. "He barely hangs on. He has a small herd that he sells to the army for beef, and a few horses. He drinks heavy and doesn't pay well. His ranch hands are bums and low-lifes. We could do without him on the plateau, but he got the land from his father and we're stuck with him." Henry walked away muttering to himself.

"Don't worry, Miss Annabella," said Charlie, "Billy always has some complaint. We just ignore him."

The kids had scrambled from the loft once the cowboy disappeared. Patrick had his arm around his sister. Toby and Skeeter walked at his back much as Charlie and Manuel had showed support and protection for Henry. Annabella smiled to herself. Her children were growing together as a fine family. Each day they claimed more of her heart.

"Is everything all right?" Patrick asked.

"I think so," said Annabella. "Charlie says that the visitor is usually cranky and complaining. But I'm glad you kept the children out of sight."

"That's what Manuel told me to do."

"And you do it every time you see that ass," Manuel said as he patted the youngster on the shoulder showing his approval. "And you make sure he and his cowboys stay away from Miss Annabella and your sisters." Patrick nodded.

xxx

As soon as Dell heard through trail gossip that Billy had been raising cane at Henry's he raced over to check on Annabella and the children. He knew something was wrong when he walked into the cabin. Dinner was usually lively and joyful. This evening everyone was quiet. Byron was huddled again Annabella, not even eating. Missy sat close to Patrick and Henry was pacing the room in a thunderous silence.

"What did that loud-mouth say?" he demanded as he slammed the door.

Henry gave him a razor-sharp look. "That fool thinks I stopped the north branch. He came here and scared everyone. Look at my babies." He threw a hand toward Byron.

"We told the boys to protect the others if Billy and his crew come back again," said Charlie. "He was his usual stupid self. How can we stop that water?"

Dell tried to stay calm and listen to what was being said. "He says the north branch is stopped?"

"No," said Henry, "He seems to think I've reduced the flow. It does seem a little sluggish. But I haven't done anything. Let's finish the grass harvest. Maybe we can send Charlie or Running Elk into the mountains to see if he can find a problem."

Running Elk nodded. "I go two days."

Dell smiled at everyone. "Problem solved. Running Elk will see what's happening. We'll tell Billy. He'll back off." Dell snapped his fingers showing how the problem would disappear. He scooted Missy down the bench and sat at the table. Everyone seemed to sigh in relief and began to attack dinner.

After the meal Dell took Annabella out for their usual quiet visit. They were both too restless to sit on the bench. "Let's walk," he suggested.

"Yes," she agreed. "That incident today made me very concerned. Will he be back to cause trouble?"

"I hope not," replied Dell. "He's a fool, but he should know that water is a big issue with statehood. Henry wouldn't be allowed to do anything to stop Double B getting water." Dell held Annabella's hand as they walked. "It's really complex, all the ideas they're arguing, but it sounds like it should be fair."

Annabella looked at him and smiled. "I don't think I want to hear complex. Just tell me my children are safe."

"I can only say that you make sure they listen to Henry or Charlie if Billy comes here again."

"Today they sent the children to hide in the barn."

"We'll be here finishing the grass and then Running Elk will investigate the problem. It could be a landslide with some boulders holding things up or some trees that fell. We'll figure it out. Two or three days, that's all we need."

This evening as they walked around the ranch, he stopped in the shadows and embraced her. It was a bold step, but she was frightened, and he felt helpless to do more. To his surprise she settled into his arms and seemed to draw strength from the closeness. When they parted, he kissed her on the nose. "Be careful. We'll figure this out."

CHAPTER 19

The shouts of fire were very confusing to Annabella. She remembered Dell's talk of lightning fires, but the grasses were harvested and the land damp from an early wet, snow. There was the shout again.

"Fire!"

She rushed from her room and ran into Morning Flower who said, "Fire in the barn. Henry has gone out."

The boys tumbled down from the loft pulling on trousers. "Smoke?" asked Patrick.

"Go see if you can help," said Annabella. The three boys slipped into their boots and ran to the door.

Henry raced into the cabin stopping Patrick at the door. "You, Skeeter and Molly get those horses. Toby you help the women with these youngsters." It was an emergency and all the children obeyed.

"I'll get them ready," promised the strategic thinker.

Henry turned to the women. "This is a set fire. Someone is trying to burn us out. Protect those small ones." He grabbed his rifle and raced back to the ranch yard.

Annabella ran to her bedroom and found Molly already dressed and ready to follow Henry's order. Missy was just waking up. Annabella helped her into clothing and finished dressing herself.

Willow came into the cabin panicked about her children's safety. Morning Flower spoke to her in their native tongue while Annabella made certain the kids were all accounted for.

"Toby, I want you to take everyone to the root cellar." He had returned from the loft with Byron in his arms and Willow's sons following. She tousled his hair. "Keep them safe and quiet. Don't come out until we come for you." He nodded. She took comfort in knowing she was talking to the strategist in the group. They pulled up the cellar door. As he helped the youngsters down, Morning Flower and Willow handed down blankets, an oil lantern and a pail of water. As an afterthought they also included a chamber pot.

Once the children were hidden, Annabella asked, "Why would someone try to burn down the barn?" She struggled to buckle her belt as she slipped on her boots.

Morning Flower knew this woman deserved more than a shrug. "Henry think it that Billy fellow." The old squaw had slipped into her daytime tunic. "We must help."

Annabella thought of Running Elk taking off this morning to research the water problem. This meant that they were one man short to fight the fire. Morning Flower was right, the women had to help. There was more shouting outside.

"No lights in cabin," whispered Morning Flower as she doused the lantern and banked the stove and slipped out into the dark night. Annabella and Willow followed Morning Flower into the chaos.

xxx

In the yard, Charlie and Manuel had gotten the horses out of the barn. They feared the chickens might be a loss. As the youngsters rushed to help, Charlie placed one on each of the horses. "Ride to Dell's and get help." He had no time to saddle the animals and was grateful the kids were skilled riders. Patrick took off while Molly and Skeeter drove the other horses ahead of them encouraging them to follow Patrick on the big bay. The chicken dog raced beside them.

Once they got out onto the field, Patrick signaled Molly to take the lead and he joined Skeeter in the rear controlling the livestock. He saw the light from Dell's ranch house and thought he heard shouting. It was Molly calling that there were riders up ahead. He raced forward to protect his sister in case the fire-starters were coming for them. But another shout stopped him.

"Patrick, it's Will. What's going on?"

"A fire."

"Someone set it," offered Skeeter as he pulled his horse to Will's side.

"We got the horses out," said Molly as she and Patrick, astride, danced around the riderless animals.

"Take them to our corral and then come back to Henry's," shouted Will as he took off. Behind him came Dell and their ranch hands. The kids did as ordered, getting the animals calmed and watered before going back to help Henry.

xxx

The women carried brooms and other implements as they raced to help save the barn. There were shadows of men working to suppress the fire and other shadows looked as though they were working to abet the flames. Annabella rushed forward, but Willow saw a familiar shape and gasped causing Annabella to halt.

Willow's eyes were wide with terror. "The animal," she whispered. Annabella saw a burly man punch Manuel and run toward the back of the cabin with a torch. Willow ran after him. Annabella followed but lost them as the riders from Dell's ranch cut across her path. Once the horses and riders moved toward the barn, she scanned the area, but couldn't find Willow. She knew they had run toward the back of the cabin so she ran in that direction.

She dashed into the darkness and bumped into the man. His torch was gone and there was no sign of Willow. Annabella feared that he had already killed the woman and was unprepared when he grabbed her and pulled her to the ground.

"I lost that Indian bitch, but I got me someone else." He pulled at Annabella's shirt, ripping the buttons and exposing her chest. He swore

112

when he realized she was wearing trousers. He pulled her arms over her head with one hand and grabbed at the waistband to pull the trousers off with his other. Cursing he pulled at her leather belt and brass buckle as Annabella struggled. Straddling her hips to keep her from moving, he slapped her with one hand while still holding her hands above her head with the other.

There was pandemonium in the yard. Shouting, animals in a panic. As she struggled, she was confused by the shadows and noise. The cabin hid her from the fire and the cowboys. She stiffened. Her attacker was distracted at something tightening around his neck. His shirt? A trail kerchief? He released her arms and grabbed at his throat. A warmth spread across her torn shirt and exposed abdomen.

Then the man slumped to the ground beside her, his eyes staring at her. Willow stood over him with a bloody knife in her hand. The noise and the shouting at the fire had hidden this drama from the other men. Annabella scrambled to her feet and knew she was looking at a new woman. Willow had avenged herself.

The women stood frozen but jumped at the sound of gunfire. Who had started shooting? Did someone see the knifing and want retribution for the death? No. The shooting was down at the barn. As the women tried to make sense of the gunfire, Will came running from the other side of the cabin. "Did you see -?" He looked at the women. He looked at the man on the ground. Even in the dark he could tell the man was dead. He saw the pale moonlight pick up the glint of Willow's knife.

"What happened?"

"This man attacked me, and Willow stopped him." Annabella was surprised at how coherent and calm she sounded. She pulled the torn pieces of her bloody shirt close about her.

Will examined the man. "He the one who-?" Willow nodded. "You cut his throat like you clean a deer. Good job. Real fast." He moved closer to Annabella. "I'm going to get my horse and I'll move his body."

"He tie horse at well," said Willow. She pointed into the darkness near the smokehouse. More random gunshots.

Will looked in that direction and saw the animal dancing at the tether disturbed by the gunshots. "I'll take care of him and his horse. When

I leave, you get in the house and get that bloody shirt off - throw it out." Annabella nodded.

Will returned with the horse in a matter of seconds. The women helped load the body on the horse. He ran to the front of the cabin and found his mount. Returning to the women he grabbed the lines of the dead man's horse and raced along with his mount for the caves. More of Henry's friends had arrived and soon the guns were silent. Once the other ranchers on the plateau had seen the fire, they had all raced to the ranch. And the raiders were subdued. Some were captured while others melted into the night.

Annabella and Willow dashed into the house to find clean clothing. After changing they ran down to the barn and threw the bloody clothes into the remaining flames. As they pulled back from the fire they saw Morning Flower bent over a body. She was sobbing. "It's Henry." The three women pulled, dragged and carried him into the cabin. He was grumbling and cursing and demanding that he get back to the fray. They finally got him into bed and allowed Morning Flower to undress him as they prepared water and cloth for bandages.

"He has wound. Bullet," said the old woman.

Annabella pulled back the blanket as he protested and found that the wound was in his stomach. She ran to find Charlie whom she thought had some experience with gunshot wounds. Willow and Morning Flower began to clean the wound.

Annabella raced around in the starlit yard to find the black man. She stopped as fear seemed to paralyze her. She recognized it as hysteria and pulled herself together. This was no time to dwell on the terror of the last few minutes. Henry needed help. "Charlie," she shouted, and he appeared, sweaty and even blacker than his normal color.

"What?" His shirt was torn and there were burn holes in his trousers.

"Someone shot Henry," she explained. "He's in the cabin. We need you." Charlie was already racing to his friend.

xxx

Will galloped into the hills tugging the dead man and his horse. He heard other horses coming toward him. They were in front of him.

He hoped that meant he wasn't being followed by the dead man's friends. Slowing he moved into shadows of a granite overhang. The moon was bright in the rugged hills and nothing could hide on the landscape. Six horses drew up to his hiding place. A man spoke the Indian language, and Will said, "Hell, Yellow Coyote, you scared the shit out of me."

The lead Indian dismounted and walked over to inspect the dead man. "He hurt Willow."

"And Willow hurt him," said Will. He heard agreeing grunts and epithets from the other braves. "Did he come to the hills often?"

"He look for gold. Come alone. Always bad. Want to make trouble."

The braves controlled the ponies who were eager to move and anxious to get away from the smell of death. "He always fight. Threaten us. He take Willow at water pool. He give us some supplies to be quiet."

One of the younger braves said, "Running Elk angry, but we worry about tribe."

"It's over," said Will. "Willow solved her problem. She stopped him from attacking Annabella."

The braves spoke among themselves. "We come for Henry. To help with fire."

"I think it's under control. The other ranchers saw the fire and came to help," explained Will, "besides there's shooting and I don't want you blamed for anything."

Yellow Coyote started to argue, "Henry is friend."

"I got a way you can help." Will considered the body. "You take this fellow and drop him in a cave. Send his horse back in a few days. I'll say I saw him run off when the shooting started."

The Indians conferred quietly. "We help with plan. Morning Flower say Henry's daughter good."

With that agreement, Will dismounted and made certain that the body was secure on the horse. He handed the leads to one of the braves, remounted and left them in the shadows as he raced back to the ranch.

xxx

The raid on the ranch was over. Dell and his ranch hands had arrived before the barn could be destroyed. The other ranchers had arrived as the shooting began and helped end the exchange. Dell did an inspection of the farm yard and walked into the cabin to assess damages there. The sky was hinting morning as the sun teased the horizon.

Things were atumble in the cabin. Annabella were tending scrapes and bruises of the ranchers while Willow prepared breakfast. He could already smell the coffee brewing.

Dell asked Annabella, "Where's Running Elk?"

"He went off to find the problem with the water yesterday morning."

Willow nodded. "He say he be gone two day."

"He'll be back soon," prophesied Dell. "If he saw the fire, he's burning leather to get back." Willow gasped and ran outside to look for her husband.

Dell pulled at Annabella's arm and dragged her closer to the lantern light. He studied her face and lightly brushed the growing bruise. "What happened to you?"

"I'll tell you later. Who else is injured?"

Dell was not happy with her reply, but he said, "I think you've seen everybody that needs tending." He walked her out into the yard.

"Where's Molly?" Annabella scanned the dark shadows in the ranch yard.

Dell laughed softly. "She collected all the rest of the livestock and has them in that corral Henry keeps for his milk cows." The rest of the livestock included an old mule, three goats, four pigs and the old chicken dog. He looked over the mess and wondered how bad it would look in full daylight. "She got the bigger animals settled and is collecting chickens now."

Even Annabella grinned at that image.

"I found some eggs," Molly called dashing toward them with an old pail lined with straw. "Some of the chickens didn't get killed. And some eggs were hidden in the mud we made with the water." She was a mess - mud, straw, ashes. And her eyes sparkled from the excitement of the evening. "We won!"

Dell took the pail from her and gave her a quick hug. Once the shooting had started he had worried about the safety of the children. "Take these to the kitchen. It'll be breakfast." She dashed off.

Dell looked around the farmyard as he and Annabella continued to assess the damage. "I can't find Will. Last I saw he was running after a fellow that slugged him and then I saw him with his horse." He stopped talking because Annabella stopped walking.

"He's gone to the mountains," she whispered.

Dell moved closer and put an arm around her. "Why?" he asked just as softly.

"A man attacked me and Willow stabbed him." Dell pulled her to his chest, and she rested her head. Finally allowing the fear inside to escape, she took a shuddering breath. "He was the man who raped Willow. She killed him when he attacked me. Will took the body away."

"The bruises?" He felt her nod her head into his chest. He took a deep breath and continued to hold her as he softly kissed her temple and caressed the bruise on her cheek. Finally, he said, "We'll wait for Will to come back before we say anything." She nodded and they walked back into the cabin. It was quiet. They could hear Morning Flower whispering and Henry arguing, but no other sounds. "Where are the little children?" asked Dell.

Annabella gasped as she fell onto a bench. "They're in the root cellar. At least that's where I left them." She heard Dell lift the trap door and then shout.

"It's me. Stop that!"

She rushed to his side and found him scraping something off his shirt. But he was smiling. "They were ready to defend themselves."

The children climbed out of the cellar. They were dirty and frightened. But seeing Annabella and Dell brought some calm to their eyes. "We thought you were the bad men," said Missy as she helped one of the small Indian boys out of the trap door. "Toby made us ready to wrap the invaders."

"Repel," Toby corrected as he pushed Byron up the ladder. "We were going to throw potatoes and apples."

"Good thinking, young fella," Dell praised the youngster. "I guess reading those stories gave you some ideas."

Toby hung his head, probably reminded of all the times he complained about having to read and study history and Greek classics. "Yes, sir." Dell laughed.

CHAPTER 20

As the sky lightened, the other ranchers assessed the damage and began to clean out the ruined walls of the barn and estimate what could be repaired and what had to be rebuilt. All the injuries had been tended and the stock accounted for. But Dell hadn't seen Will since Annabella explained his disappearance into the mountains. Maybe he was hurt and laid up somewhere in those mountains. As he did another sweep of the yard, Dell noted that there was no evidence of the man Willow had murdered. Dell shivered. If the body turned up, it would be a challenge to keep suspicion away from the Indians. He did a diligent and thorough search of the grounds but was unable to find the knife. He was glad Running Elk was off on the water search.

Maybe Willow still had the knife. Dell knew he would feel better if he had it. He heard a horse at gallop, then he saw the rider. Within minutes he recognized Will. "Where have you been?" demanded Dell, relieved to finally see his brother.

"I helped a body find his salvation." Will slid from his horse and brushed dirt from his clothing.

Dell looked confused.

"Did Annabella tell you?" asked Will. In the morning light he looked exhausted.

Dell nodded and thought about a question. "You buried him?"

"I helped him into the ground."

"You know the coyotes will dig him up. You didn't have time to bury him deep."

Will pulled his horse along toward the water trough. "I didn't bury anybody. I saw him go off toward those caves, probably looking for gold." Then Will grinned. "If anyone finds his horse, they'll probably find a few nuggets in the saddle bags." He dusted the mountain dirt from his leggings. "You know you shouldn't go in those caves alone, a fellow who doesn't want to share his gold could end up in real trouble."

"His horse?" Dell wondered how much he wanted to know. "When will they find the horse?"

"Running Elk's tribe will release him in three days to find his way home with a few nuggets in his saddle bags. They don't want Running Elk and his family to return to the tribe. They're still worried the law will catch up." Will slapped his brother on the back. "How about some breakfast?"

xxx

By midmorning Dell and the other ranchers had organized their crews to do what repairs they could. Molly had all the farm animals in protective corrals. Charlie and Manuel were a little angry, but impressed, with her solution for the chickens. She had managed to save over half the flock and she secured them in the bunkhouse. Or as Manuel was heard to say, "Shit house now."

One of the other ranchers stopped laughing long enough to point out that she was a pretty smart youngster. He also said, "The faster we get the coops up the faster you can reclaim your bed." Charlie and Manuel understood that. But they knew that the barn needed repairs first. Everything depended on getting it ready for winter - snow would be there soon.

Orville from the Bar Eight asked the crowd, "What do we do about Double B? They attacked Henry and could have killed some of us." They had Billy and three of his hands tied up and locked in Henry's tool shed.

Will said, "We should take Old Billy," the Double B owner, "into town and let the sheriff and the judge deal with things."

"If he gets handed over, who gets the ranch?" asked Simon from the Double X. "He got no kin that we know of."

Dell cleared his throat and said, "I have an idea." He addressed Simon and Orville. "We all touch Double B, Maybe we can offer some money to the court to cover fines or things and each take a portion of the ranch."

Orville cleared his throat. "I got a better idea. Let's keep the judge out of this. We can buy the ranch from Billy today." Billy could be heard shouting from the tool shed. The rancher ignored the shouts, "And we can split the land and make Billy use that money to pay Henry for all the damage." He threw his arm out to call attention to the destruction.

"That's a better idea," said Simon. "You know that judge might just sell the land to his cousin or some other fool." Everyone had a comment to make about the judge's cousin.

"All right," agreed Dell, "Let's talk land and money." He took a stick and drew an outline of the ranch lands and added certain geological characteristics. "Let's decide on a price and think about it. We gotta be fair or the judge might just not accept it, saying Billy needs money for his defense."

"I got one more idea." Orville cleared his throat. "We all buy the portion we want. Make Billy pay Henry." He looked slyly at the other ranchers. "Then we send him and his remaining men off this plateau. We don't call any law."

"He won't have money to pay the men. Those fellows will -

Orville nodded, not trying to conceal his sly smile. "Save us all time and no one has to go into town when we got a lot to do before winter."

Dell and Simon were silent as they thought about the idea. Orville continued to list his arguments. "He needs money. He probably owes his hands back pay. Henry needs money for rebuilding and doesn't have any more time than we have to go to a trial. Billy might survive a trial because some lawyer might argue that with all the confusion nobody can be sure of anything."

More thinking. Finally, they all nodded in silent agreement. Billy would ride off the plateau.

The three men began their discussion of money and land even as they directed the cowboys on the work to be done. By the end of the day, they felt they had reached a reasonable dollar figure and determined which rancher was best situated to buy which portion of the ranch. The final discussion revolved around the actual ranch house, outbuildings and surrounding acreage.

Dell had plans for Annabella and the children. He had thought about finding other property for Will because Will needed his own portion. They could be partners in the big spread, but he needed a home so he could build a family. Dell cleared his throat. "Will and I want to buy the buildings and livestock." The other two men looked at him.

"You got that much money?"

"I do," said Dell. He was already buying the largest portion of ranch lands. Orville and Simon had both wanted only the acreage closest to their own ranches.

"It's yours." Simon closed the deal.

"Now we just settle on guarding Billy until tomorrow morning," said Dell. "The rest of his ranch hands are out there somewhere." The other ranchers nodded. "They want their money, but they don't want to hang for the fire." The guards were posted.

That evening they met with Billy and explained life. They would give him letters for the bank in town. One rider from each ranch would go with him into town and see that all the papers were drawn correctly. Simon and Orville each sent a son and Dell volunteered Will.

Billy replied, "Just give me two days before you let those cowboys know what we did."

The next morning four men rode out. Will and the two sons were to return with the deeds and the money that was owed Henry. By noontime three men returned and Double B hands who had been watching from the ridge became suspicious as the Double B hands still in the tool shed were released. The ranchers were too calm. No one was chasing them. Billy had disappeared. Maybe he escaped.

The released cowboys and those on the ridge soon joined forces. As the ranchers watched the riders gallop toward town, Simon said, "They figured it out."

Dell nodded. "Not all of them ran. Maybe there's some good cowboys in the bunch." He watched three Double B cowboys approach the barn - an older man and two young men who looked a few years older than Patrick. "You work for Billy?" Dell asked.

The older man was the spokesman. "We be here only two months."

Dell caught the lilt of an accent, not unusual on the open range. "Where you from?"

"Me and my boys come from north. Our water dry up. My wife and daughter work in town. We don't set fire. We argue with boss, he tell us to go to hell."

"Where'd the rest of the crew go?" Dell could just see their dust.

"They say Billy owe us pay. I think Billy cheat us. Me and my boys looking for a better boss."

Dell thought about his life on the plateau. His folks had built a fine spread and a good life for him and Will. He had learned from others their stories of trials and hardship and he knew that he was a very lucky man. He studied the old cowpoke with the accent and with the thinning blond hair and his two healthy sons. "I just bought part of the Double B. And I bought the buildings and the livestock for me and my brother. You want a job?"

"Me and my boys?"

Dell took off his hat and slapped it on his knee watching ashes and a few chicken feathers flutter to the ground. "You and your family move into Billy's house and manage my portion of the ranch."

"My women, too?"

"Yeah. We need more women here to make us civilized." Dell thought for a moment. "But stay here for a few days and help fix this place."

The old cowboy nodded then went off to share the good news with his sons while Dell headed into the house to let Henry know what had been decided.

xxx

Running Elk had watched the fire from the hills two nights ago. He had been too far in the hills to get to the ranch. As he watched he saw the fire disappear and relaxed, thinking all was under control. But on his return, he learned the truth. He had talked with the other tribe members as they disposed of a body. Willow had avenged herself and saved Annabella according to the report he received. Today he was coming back to the ranch. His wife had seen him arrive and rushed to speak with him. He nodded to her and said in his quiet voice using his tribal dialect that he understood what had happened.

Dell saw the man and called to him. "Did you find out what the problem is?"

Running Elk turned his attention to the rancher who looked exhausted. "Several large boulders have fallen. Stream must make new path."

"Do you think the stream will come back to capacity or do we have to go up there and blast it or something?"

Running Elk smiled at Dell. "It not matter. Willow say all land belong to you."

"I did buy part of the Double B." Dell rubbed his eyes. "But we still need that water."

The Indian understood. "It come back. Water washing dirt away. Make new path."

"Thank you," said Dell. "Get yourself some breakfast. We've got a lot of work to do here."

xxx

Once the division of the Double B was settled, Dell sent Running Elk, Patrick, Toby and two of his ranch hands out to collect the winter hay that was baled in the fields while directing some of the ranchers to reenforce a makeshift chicken coop. Annabella and Willow were preparing dinner for everyone while Missy tended the little children.

Morning Flower refused to leave Henry's bedside.

As she brought in kindling for the stove Molly gasped at the sight of the dirty children. Even though she was filthy herself, she grabbed a cloth and began to wipe each small face. Dell, who had stepped into the house to check on Henry and the children, noticed that she was learning how to take responsibility for all of them just like Annabella.

Charlie came over to Annabella. "I done all I know. It's a bad wound for an old man." There were tears in his eyes.

Henry called for Dell and Annabella. They rushed to his side. The man had a deep wound and the smoke he had inhaled saving his livestock and barn had taken a toll. Morning Flower had cleaned his face and taken the sooty clothing away. She even had opened the window, but nothing seemed to clear Henry's lungs.

He gestured for his two visitors to move closer. "I deeded my farm to Annabella," he whispered, then coughed. "Dell, you marry her and add my land to yours. I woudda sold it to you but I didn't need the money." Cough.

Annabella took Henry's hand, tears in her eyes, "Henry, what are you saying?"

"You're my only kin." More coughing, reaching for air that was elusive. "My boy said you were a good woman. And you gave me a family." Coughing and a sip of water. "The ranch is yours. That lawyer in town knows."

Annabella couldn't speak. All the emotion that she had held at bay forced itself out - tears and great sobs. She ran from the room. Dell stepped in closer to Henry. "I'll take care of all of them, even Morning Flower and her kin. You just rest up."

xxx

Henry struggled to breathe as he turned toward the squaw once they were alone. "All these years I never knew your name was Morning Flower. That's real pretty." He was having trouble with each breath. "I wasn't mean to you, was I?"

"You were always kind and I had enough to eat." She took his hand. "Thank you, Henry."

"You never said my name before."

"I am pleased to say it now. You are good man."

Later in the day Annabella found Morning Flower sitting on an old chair, holding Henry's hand. When she entered the bedroom, the older woman said, "He passed." Tears ran down the wrinkles in her face, along the route they had traveled for many years when she had cried for all the others who had left her behind.

CHAPTER 21

It was days before Dell and Annabella found time to talk alone. Henry had been laid to rest. The barn had been reasonably repaired. The other ranchers had returned to their own spreads offering to return when needed. And life in the cabin had settled down.

Charlie and Manuel had cleared the chickens out of the bunkhouse, moving them into new quarters, and Annabella was getting everyone back into their lessons. In fact, the other ranchers had hinted that their children would benefit from some reading and cyphers. Annabella suggested that they let her give some thought to how she could manage. They were content with that half promise because everyone saw how she sparkled when she talked about teaching more youngsters. They knew she would make it happen.

"I hear you're starting a school." Dell opened their conversation as they walked to the bench at the back of the garden. He had studied her face during dinner and saw that the bruises inflicted during the attempted rape were turning yellow and fading. He took a deep breath, saying a silent prayer of thanksgiving to whomever was listening that she had been protected and defended by Willow.

Winter was coming. It was almost too cold for a quiet time in the garden. Annabella sat on the bench wrapped in a heavy blanket and looked up at him. He couldn't resist. He bent, gave her a soft kiss, pulled back, smiled and sat beside her. "A lot has happened," he said. It took her a moment to recover from the surprise of his kiss.

"That's an understatement," she replied. "Henry's dead. I own a ranch. He also left me money." She paused and thought. Then said, "I have more money."

"More money?"

She smiled a secret smile. Dell could only see half of her face. "I have money in the bank in town. I've always saved my earnings and didn't spend much. It's added up."

"Added up?"

"I think I had enough to cover the repairs even if that man hadn't paid us for the ruin."

Dell took her hand. "When we marry, you should keep that as your own." He kissed her hand.

"We never got to tell him that we planned to marry." Annabella added that to the regrets of her life.

"He suspected something," said Dell, caressing her hand. "He fixed this bench up so I could court you." She smiled at him.

"I've been thinking," she replied. "I want so many things for the children. And I'll need help with this ranch. I could use a husband."

"That doesn't sound complementary to me," he said, brushing her knuckles with his fingertips.

"I don't mean it as an insult, Dell. You're a fine man. But I've been married. I've given this a lot of thought. I may not be a good wife. I don't have any passion."

"Passion?"

"I had married relations with my husband." She sighed searching for the words. "I never felt, well, felt like the novels say I should."

He thought about that. "Maybe he didn't try hard enough."

"Oh, yes," she assured him, "every Saturday night. He was kind and even tried to encourage me. I think it was me. I'm deficient."

Dell thought about all the many ways he had seen her - brave, strong, sad, but very reserved. He remembered the phrase Henry had used, she guarded her heart. He took that as a challenge. He would find her heart. And, by golly, lovemaking wouldn't just be reserved for Saturday night.

But tonight he didn't want to scare her. He said, "I want to help you with those youngsters. I've grown fond of them. I also want to have a partner so I'm not alone in my old age. I think we can work well together."

Annabella thought. "I agree. As long as you know I'm deficient."

He nodded in return. "We can marry at Christmas. The farm work is not as demanding then."

xxx

Once she accepted Dell's marriage plans, Annabella wrote to her brother. It was a long and difficult letter but prompted by the joy she found in her future. She remembered the early years of her childhood when she and her brother had shared games and teased one another. He might not respond, but she had to write.

Dell took her letter into town one day saying he would take a pack horse and get some final supplies before the worst part of the winter set in. He invited Toby and Skeeter along for the trail ride. They took Henry's old mule and also one that Dell kept at his farm. As he explained, "Our horses may have some trouble, but these old fellows never miss a step."

The boys were so excited, and the journey met their expectations. The landscape was a winter dream - frozen waterfalls, long views unobstructed by greenery, and lost livestock. As they related their stories, Dell had to explain, "We helped an old rancher near town who had not locked his barn. His milk cow got out and went looking for food."

To which Skeeter added, "We found her eating old grass where we picnicked on that day when we found you."

"And Dell was right about those old mules," chimed in Toby. "They just walked. They didn't even look at the scenery."

There were two trails onto the plateau, one was the wagon trail they had used in their first days. The other was a longer way but with less steep grades. That was the trail they had used with the mules. "Why don't we use that trail?" asked Annabella.

"It goes too close to Double B and sometimes Billy shoots at wagons, saying he thinks we're stealing." He stopped and grinned.

"But it's ours now!" they all said at once.

Dell nodded his head. "Correct. I guess in the spring we can get Will to start working on making it wider for wagons." They all agreed because wagon rides on the steep trail could get hair-raising at times.

There would be a lot of changes in the spring - new marriage, new house, new family, and a new trail.

CHAPTER 22

After finalizing all the deeds and paperwork for the land purchase and settlement of the Double B, as well as seasonal snowfalls, it was a few weeks before Dell and Will were finally able to inspect the ranch buildings they had purchased. The Double B ranch house was a one-story stone and log structure that sort of leaned toward a sorry looking kitchen garden. "I guess Billy didn't work too hard to keep up appearances," commented Will as he tripped over a broken bucket buried in the snow.

"He lived here alone," Dell observed. "I never heard talk of women or family."

Will snorted. "He never washed. What woman would stand for that?" The young cowpoke pushed open the cabin door. Something ran across the floor and out into the sunshine. "A cat! Wonder how long he'd been waiting to escape." Both men sniffed the unmistakable odors of male cat.

"A long time," guessed Dell. He walked back outside for some fresh air. "Let me tell you my plan."

Will smiled at his brother. "You want to be alone with your new wife, and all those youngsters so you bought me a house." Dell blushed and Will hooted his delight. "And you bought me a cat so I won't get lonely."

"A little more than that," said Dell with some caution, causing Will to get serious. "We'll be telling the kids soon about our plans. I want us all organized." Dell continued, "I invited those Swedes who stayed behind to help when Billy ran off - that old man and his two sons. I said they could live here and manage this place and work for us since we now have another thousand or so acres with this land and Henry's place."

"So where do I live?"

"You can stay with me and Annabella and those youngsters." Dell slapped his brother on the back. "One more youngster won't make us any difference." He stared off toward the horizon for a few minutes. "Will, we got the makings of a good ranch and family business. I bought these buildings so that you can start thinking about a family and make a homestead here." Dell threw his arm to encompass the ranch yard and surrounding land. "We can build you a home and we'll be close by and work our land and raise our families." Dell was silent as the future danced before him - sons, daughters, nieces and nephews.

Will draped an arm around his brother's shoulders. "I can see it all with you." He spoke in a soft affectionate tone. "I guess I got to find me a wife." He slapped Dell on the back.

They turned as they heard a wagon approach. It wheeled down from the ridge and rattled into the yard. Three very blond people occupied the wagon and two blond horsemen trotted behind. "Ay, Mr. Dell," called the old man driving the wagon. "I bring my family to our new home."

Two tall, broad, young blond men climbed down from their horses and stood before the Rutherford brothers. "My boys, Lars and Gunner you already know. And," he gestured to himself, "me, Ake." He turned to the two women climbing down from the wagon. "My wife, Freja, and my daughter," Dell heard Will gasp as a beautiful young woman leaped gracefully from the back of the wagon, "she is Astrid." Will rushed to greet the women and Dell shook hands with Ake. The sons stood like formidable guards, protecting the family.

"Ake," said Dell, "I'm pleased we could work this out. My brother and I were just inspecting the cabin. Your women might find it harsh. They might want to stay in town until things are cleaner."

Freja walked to stand beside her husband. "We come now. I don't like the men in town looking at Astrid." Dell didn't comment but he could understand, because Will was having difficulty being coherent in Astrid's presence. He hoped the brothers didn't break Will's legs or some other body part to keep him from falling all over the young woman.

Ake watched as his sons drew closer to Will. "I think we sleep in the bunkhouse for a bit. My boys and I kept it clean. Mama would be angry if we be sloppy." They all looked toward the single storied structure situated halfway between the barn and the dilapidated ranch house. It didn't look in much better condition than the house.

The tired draft horses shuffled and snorted shifting the wagon which appeared to be stuffed with furniture and other belongings. Freja announced, "You boys," here she included Will, "take our things to Papa's bunkhouse." She watched another cat step out of the cabin. "Astrid, you open windows and air out Papa's bunkhouse."

"Mama," moaned Ake, "it's clean. We learned from the best." He kissed her cheek, and she gave him a push as she giggled and blushed.

Upon inspection the men determined that the unhappy cowpokes who had been abandoned by Billy had returned to the ranch to claim their possessions before leaving the plateau. As they departed, they had broken windows and stoved in doors at the bunkhouse. They also left a pile of broken furniture and scattered pieces of an old heating stove.

Freja joined the men as they stared at the destruction. "Papa, you get your tools. We begin to make our home." And Dell watched as Freja organized the family's new life. With a wave she signaled that the wagon be moved. "Lars, take the wagon to unload at the barn. See to the animals. Astrid and Gunner, clean out the bunk house so Papa can begin his work." The family acted on Mama's instructions.

Will watched Astrid move as Dell elbowed him. "Those brothers are mighty big. You better keep your eyes in your head."

"She is a beauty." As innocently as possible Will said, "I'll help them settle and inspect the rest of the buildings. I'll be home for dinner." Dell tried not to laugh out loud at his transparent brother.

He turned to Ake. "You let my brother know what supplies you need for the buildings. And we'll talk in a few days about our work schedule." The old man waved his understanding and turned to follow Mama's orders. Dell slapped Will's shoulder, swung onto his horse and rode from the ranch yard as he listened to Freja give orders like a general.

CHAPTER 23

It was four weeks since the raid and Henry's burial. Today was the day that Dell and Annabella would tell the family of their plans. They had been quiet all this time because there were so many things, so many people, to consider. Ranch hands, children, Indians - how had Annabella's life gotten so complicated, so full, she wondered.

All the children, the Indians and the ranch hands were gathered in Henry's cabin. Annabella had indicated that there was to be a ranch meeting before Sunday dinner.

"A ranch meeting?" asked Molly. "What's that?"

"They're going to send us away," sniffed Skeeter.

"Why?" asked Missy. "We behave and do our chores." Soon five children were crying and Patrick the oldest was looking miserable.

"Where can we seat everyone?" asked Annabella as she breezed through the room with an extra stool. She was challenged to find enough benches and chairs.

"You don't want us," sobbed Missy. "When do we have to leave?"

Finally, Annabella noticed the children's tears. She dropped to her knees and hugged Missy. Byron intruded in the hug, just to make certain he wasn't forgotten. "This is a happy meeting. I want you all to let the adults have seats and then you can pull up the bench and crates. Dell and I have an announcement."

Molly rolled her eyes in teenage sophistication. "We all know you're courting."

Dell came up behind her and lifted her onto a bench. "You think you know everything, just because you're so pretty." She blushed.

"I'm pretty, too," announced Missy.

"Me, too," said Byron.

Before Missy could turn and explain to the little fellow that only girls were pretty, Dell took control of the first ever ranch meeting. Clearing his throat, he said, "I guess no one will be surprised when Annabella and I tell you we plan to marry." Cheers and giggles filled the room. He pushed the air down with his hands indicating that he wanted silence. "We know that it's going to be a change for us and that it may be a change for everyone. We have some ideas and want to see if you all agree." Everyone nodded. Even Willow and Running Elk were interested in this discussion. They had heard rumors that the Indian Affairs people were looking for strays. "Listen to our ideas and then have your say." Dell began to pace in front of the group wondering how Annabella could stand in front of students all day and talk. He was certain he didn't have that many words in him. But he began, "Annabella and I want to move to my ranch, and we want the kids to come with us. Although Annabella owns Henry's ranch, we think Morning Flower and her family can live here because she was Henry's squaw and Annabella's mother-in-law. We think we can keep you folks here," his arms swept over Running Elk and his family, "because you're related to Annabella by her marriage to Mr. Winters' son and I'll promise any government people who ask that I'll give you a job on the ranch. And Charlie and Manuel, you fellows can stay in your bunk house and train Running Elk to be a rancher."

"I want to keep my school going," said Annabella, "Dell promised to build a schoolhouse because the other ranchers want schooling, too."

"That means," said Dell, "that we want everyone to stay and work with us. Any questions?"

"What about Will?" asked Skeeter. "You didn't say his name." They all turned to look at Will who was leaning against the far wall. He grinned.

Dell smiled at Skeeter. "Will is planning on staying at our ranch." All the kids cheered at that news.

"When you marry?" asked Morning Flower. She had reached out to take Annabella's hand.

"We've still got some work to do on Dell's house," said Annabella, "and some work here to get us all ready for winter. So we will marry on Christmas Day. That's only five weeks from today."

Dell asked, "Any more questions or should we have dinner?"

"Dinner!"

It was a loud and boisterous meal. Dell and Annabella found time to step outside the kitchen door to take a breath and to share a hug. Winter was here, the afternoon was darkening, and they wouldn't be able to spend much more time on their courting bench. Dell led her to the bench at the edge of the garden, now a brown memory of the summer's bounty with scattered snow that seemed to fall in inches every day. "We told them," he said as he settled her in his arms.

She smiled. "We didn't surprise anyone." They sat quietly holding hands as had become their custom.

There was a shuffling noise and they both looked up to find Patrick nervously approaching. "Can I speak?" he asked.

"Certainly," said Annabella as she took the boy's hand. Dell rose from the bench and stood beside the youngster who in the last months had grown as tall as Will.

"I been thinking," the boy began, "I should be going out on my own. Find me a job and start taking care of myself. The young'uns are settled with you. I can be .. ah .."

"Independent?" suggested Dell.

"Free of responsibilities?" added Annabella. His face looked pained. Annabella rubbed his hands and pulled him down beside her on the bench. "Why do you want to leave us?"

He gulped, looking for air, trying to control his tears. "I'm too old."

Dell put a hand on his shoulder. "I'd be sorry to see you leave us."

"I could stay in the bunkhouse with Charlie and Manuel." Annabella pulled his head to her shoulder. "I could . ." They heard him sniffle.

"I guess you could be a ranch hand," said Dell. "I'd pay you fair. I know you work hard. I guess you have a choice. You can stay at the bunkhouse and be a ranch hand or you can come to the house and be our son." Patrick started to sob. Annabella held him.

She whispered, "You've been such a brave fellow, taking care of your brother and the girls. You work hard for the ranch and you study and are a good student. You are a young fellow we are proud of, Patrick. Can you find it in your heart to stay in our family and be our son?"

"I thought I was too big, too old." Dell handed him a kerchief. "I thought wedded folk only want small kids and their own babies."

"You're my son," said Annabella. "You have been from the day you got off that train."

"And now you'll stay our son, if you accept us," said Dell. The youngster grinned and wiped his eyes. He hugged Annabella and then stood and hugged Dell. "Why don't you check on the livestock and then come in for dessert." The boy raced toward the barn, leaving his two grinning parents behind.

CHAPTER 24

Dell and Annabella were taking a Sunday afternoon horseback ride. Byron sat in front of Dell and Missy clung behind Annabella. "I thought we should start planning your move to the house. It's on a real pretty knoll with trees to keep it cool in the summer." They were taking a leisurely ride to look over the ranch. Since Dell had suggested a Christmas wedding and Annabella had agreed, he thought they should be getting ready.

As they came around the outcropping, the house came into view. "It is a lovely setting." Annabella studied the house. It was stone and timber, with a steep roof nestling a loft or second story. Getting closer Annabella could see various additions and dormers in the roof.

"Mom always seemed to need more space. It's like she knew I would bring you and the children one day." Dell looked at the house and saw their future. "It's got five bedrooms and a big kitchen. Pop was thinking of adding an indoor bathing room and one of those toilettes that Mom saw in the mail order catalogue."

"Really?" That was the most excitement he had ever heard in her voice.

"Sounds like I got your interest."

She smiled. "An indoor privy makes you very desirable."

He laughed which caused Byron to laugh with him. "I guess you have shown me your priorities." They tied their horses to a shrub at the front of the house. Dell helped the children down and they all entered the house.

Annabella saw dusty, sparsely furnished rooms - a parlor, a dining room, a library or office room and stairs. Beyond the stairs was the kitchen Dell had bragged about. It was the room that verified human inhabitants. Will and Dell probably spent all their time in the kitchen or bedrooms. They had no need for the other spaces.

Dell showed her the water pump, the large pantry and storage areas. He pointed out the stove very similar to the one at Henry's place. The room also had a big round table, a great place for a farm breakfast, thought Annabella. Dell stepped into an alcove. "Pop planned for the bathing room in here."

He took her upstairs and showed her the room he would claim for them and a small room that he said, "might make a nursery." She blushed. Although the roof was steep, she noticed that all the rooms had windows coming out as dormers. "Why is the roof so steep?"

"It keeps the snow from building up and the roof falling in." He pointed out other features. "I think the girls can have this room. This room is Will's. And the boys can sleep here. When Will moves out we can consider other arrangements."

"When Will moves out?"

He put an arm around Annabella. "I want us to be a family and I want Will to build his own. We bought the Double B place to get him started."

"Does Will know that?"

"He does. We've talked about things." He pulled her closer. "A man likes to be alone with his wife."

Annabella stiffened, but before Dell could comment they heard laughter from below. It sounded like Byron and Missy were getting into trouble. They ran down the stairs. To their surprise, they found the two children at the big round table huddled over a mail order catalogue, giggling.

"They have pictures of women's bloomers," laughed Missy, "and men's long johns." Byron pointed and laughed, "Men."

Annabella took in a quick breath. "I haven't seen a catalog for almost a year."

"Why don't you take it back to the cabin. You might find things you need for this house. Maybe even look over that water closet device."

He picked up Byron and she picked up the catalogue and signaled to Missy that it was time to go. As they walked to the door she asked, "How long does an order take to arrive?"

Dell smiled to himself. Patience, he thought, she would become his wife and partner. She just needed to be encouraged. Placing orders for household goods might help melt her heart.

CHAPTER 25

After Dell and Annabella made their wedding announcement Manuel disappeared. When asked Charlie had no clue. "He didn't say anything to me, Miss Annabella. He was just gone when I woke this morning."

"I didn't owe him wages, did I?"

"No, ma'am," replied Charlie. "Henry paid us before the fire."

It was a puzzle, and the burden of Manuel's chores fell to Running Elk and Patrick. But ranch life continued. That evening Annabella explained their loss to Dell. "It is peculiar," he agreed, "Manuel had been here a long time. I wonder if he was lost with Henry's death?"

No one knew the answer, but life went on. Until a week later when Dell found Manuel and a woman in the Rocking R kitchen. "Mr. Dell," began Manuel, "I have woman to help Miss Annabella when she become your wife. Carmelita, my woman, can help clean and cook. She ready to cook and help clean now, get things ready for Miss Annabella."

"Ma'am," Dell nodded to the woman. "Please sit. I was just getting some breakfast. You both hungry?"

"We cook," Manuel said. "We show you Carmelita good worker." With that the two visitors bustled around the kitchen. Dell studied the woman. She was small, slender and maybe close to fifty. Her long black hair was threaded with strands of gray. Her hands looked as though they knew hard work, and her eyes were filled with sorrow. Dell knew he was looking at a woman who had known many hardships.

"What do I smell?" called Will as he came into the kitchen. He stopped abruptly, surveying the two kitchen visitors. "Manuel, we thought you ran off." He nodded to Carmelita. "Ma'am."

"Manuel has asked if I want to hire Carmelita as a cook and housekeeper. He says she could be helpful to Annabella when the children move in after the wedding."

Will slapped Manuel on the back. "That's a great idea. And I can tell you right now, she cooks better than me or Dell." Will already had a plate ready to receive the eggs and bacon in the skillet. He and Dell usually took meals at the bunkhouse with the wranglers. Grandy, the cook, had a lot of good recipes in him.

They all enjoyed breakfast and Manuel helped Carmelita clean afterward. Dell cleared his throat. "Manuel, what will you do? Stay here or go back to Henry's?"

"I stay with my woman, but I am happy to work where you tell me." He got a teasing look in his eyes. "When you marry you own all the land, both ranches."

"Annabella owns Henry's ranch. We want it to be a safe place for Morning Flower and her family, away from the government men." Dell laughed, "But you're right. I will manage both ranches. And we can use you in both places." He stood and held his hand out to Carmelita. "Ma'am, I'm happy to offer you a job at this ranch. My new family will be delighted with your cooking. Come with me and Manuel to the other ranch and I'll introduce you to my family."

Carmelita smiled. "Thank you, Mr. Dell. Manuel say you are a kind man."

"That's because you're a fine cook. Breakfast was mighty flavorful."

Manuel and Carmelita exchanged a look. He had told her that Dell was not like the other men she had met during her life who had treated her with such abuse. She would be safe here on the ranch. He and Dell would make certain.

xxx

"A cook and housekeeper?" Annabella was puzzled as Dell explained about Carmelita.

"It appears that she is Manuel's woman," Dell explained as Annabella scowled. "I don't know what else to call her. He didn't say she was his wife. But she cooks real good. Manuel's bringing her here later to meet everyone."

"Where will she stay?"

"For now we can make up a small room out of those storage pantries at the Rocking R kitchen. I suspect Manuel will come up with another solution. He just wanted to insure we hired her first."

At that moment Manuel ushered Carmelita into the cabin. Dell heard Annabella take in a breath. Annabella saw the pain and years of abuse in the woman's eyes and in the way she instinctively tried to prepare to defend herself. "She needs us."

Dell welcomed her. "Carmelita, this is our big family." He introduced everyone as best he could. "Annabella here will be my wife in a few weeks, and these are our children."

"Can you bake cookies?" asked Missy. "We don't get many cookies. Everyone is too busy."

"I like cookies," offered Byron and Carmelita smiled. Maybe for the first time in years.

CHAPTER 26

Dell and Will arrived at Annabella's cabin early Christmas morning. Dell was ready to be a groom and he was worried as he studied the sky that a blizzard might interfere with his wedding night plans. He thought he would try to hurry the preacher and the Christmas dinner and get Annabella back to his place before dark. He scowled at the sky, warning those clouds to hold off for the time being.

Will read his mind because he said to his brother, "You might spend your wedding night with all of us." He laughed. "Maybe we can make you a spot in the barn for some privacy."

"I swear I'm going to knock you on your ass if you don't shut up," growled the nervous groom. "You keep your ideas about my wedding night to yourself."

Will laughed harder. Just as they arrived at the cabin, a few big snowflakes drifted to the ground. Molly opened the door and shouted a greeting. The boys ran out to take the horses. Charlie was already tying ropes from the cabin to the bunkhouse to the barn. Folks knew that a blizzard could white out everything and a person could get lost just going to the privy.

Dell frowned. Everyone was expecting snow. He just hoped the preacher arrived. And blessedly he saw the lone horseman on the horizon. He waved. The man came into the yard and the boys took his horse. Will greeted him and led him into the house. Dell followed thinking how lucky they had been to find this traveling preacher. He had spent Christmas Eve with the other families on the plateau, agreeing to be on hand for a wedding today.

"Looks like a mighty storm," offered the preacher as he walked into the cabin. "Smells mighty good in here." The Christmas and wedding celebration would only include the immediate family - or as Annabella liked to think of them - all the folks Henry had taken in.

The cabin was decorated with pine boughs and ribbon. There was a fire going in the big stone fireplace and the cookstove was fairly brimming with pots and kettles. Morning Flower was stirring something, and Willow was dicing. Annabella was kneading more dough - in a dress. Dell had never seen her in a dress since the day she got off the train last summer.

It was a mighty pretty dress, not fancy, dark green with some lace trim. Then he realized that Molly and Missy were also in dresses. He suspected that Annabella had been working hard at Henry's sewing apparatus. The girls even had dainty shoes and ribbons in their hair. Daughters! Dell gave them both a hug and complemented them on their beauty.

Kneading the dough Annabella recalled that she had not looked forward to cooking for her family - all alone. Morning Flower and Willow would be staying here at the cabin. She and the children would be moving to Dell's ranch. Fortunately, Dell had welcomed a woman Manuel had brought to the ranch and proposed that she become household help to assist Annabella. It was an inspired idea. And today, Carmelita, Manuel's lady friend was here at the cabin to assist with the Christmas meal.

Annabella marveled that it took four grown women and two young girls to feed all of the cabin clan three meals every day. She kept kneading the dough - even on her wedding day!

As the women cooked the men prepared the large room for the wedding ceremony. According to the way Dell had organized the day, they would wed, eat and leave for his ranch, one night alone before the children moved in. On schedule the preacher performed the ceremony, everyone kissed the bride and congratulated Dell. The men then set up the room for the great Christmas Day dinner. But first, there were chores. The animals had to be tended, more wood carried in, more water heated. And to everyone's surprise, Annabella had presents for everyone. So Dell adjusted the schedule to allow everyone to open their presents.

Time for dinner and someone announced that it was really coming down. Dell stole a glance out the window and cursed to himself. It was a white world outside. No one was going anywhere this evening. Maybe he would have to take Annabella to the barn to be alone.

Morning Flower placed a roasted wild turkey on the table and Willow followed with preserved vegetables and stewed apples and potatoes and breads. There was cider, milk and butter and finally pies and hard candy. Annabella again surprised everyone with chocolate candies for one and all. The blizzard continued, but the cabin glowed with the firelight and lanterns. The cabin was a glowing yellow speck against the gray, darkening blizzard night.

And that's how he found them.

As everyone relaxed in the snug winter evening, there was a scratching at the door. An odd sound, especially when no living creature should be about. Will reached for the weapon that he had placed on the mantle. Dell approached the door as the other men prepared to defend the cabin. Willow herded the smaller children to the back bedroom.

Dell slowly opened the door and found a young Indian sprawled on the porch. He was a member of Running Elk's old tribe. Charlie and the preacher pulled him into the cabin while Dell and Will did a quick search of the yard to see if there were others.

The youngster was about Patrick's age and wearing few clothes. His feet were well wrapped in skins, but his arms were bare. Morning Flower brought blankets as he was placed on the floor in front of the fireplace. She spoke with him, placing her ear against his lips and gasped.

"There are others," she cried. "They are lost in the snows. The woman is with child. She comes here because the midwife died."

Charlie said, "We better go out now before his tracks get covered."

"We'll have to go on foot," said Dell, "That snow is too high for a horse or wagon."

With that statement, Dell gave orders to prepare some lanterns on poles and to gather blankets to take. Their goal would be to find the people lost in the blizzard and get them safely back to the cabin.

As the supplies were prepared Will scouted the yard to make certain they would know in which direction the youngster had come. "As we thought," said Will as he returned to the cabin, "he came from the caves. I don't think they'll be too hard to find. And that snow isn't as deep as we thought. Charlie, hitch that sledge you use to bring the feed to our ranch."

Charlie and Patrick dressed and hurried to the barn while Dell, Will and Running Elk dressed and walked into the night with lanterns hanging from poles. When Charlie and Patrick left the barn with two horses pulling the sledge, the old chicken dog followed.

As the men walked into the night, Morning Flower and Willow began tending to the young brave. The women explained that freezing people had to be handled in ways contrary to what one would think. Packing parts of the young man's body in snow became important. Then his limbs were rubbed, warm drinks were prepared, and he was encouraged to stay alert and not sleep.

Anticipating more people arriving, Annabella and the children began pushing tables aside and collecting more blankets and cleaning dishes and cups for the new arrivals. Annabella sent Toby and Skeeter for more wood because Morning Flower whispered that they might be delivering a baby this evening also.

Charlie drove the sledge as Patrick ran ahead to make certain they stayed on the trail blazed by the men from the cabin. He shouted back at Charlie and squinted ahead to catch a glimpse of the lanterns in the swirling snow. It looked as though the walking men had separated. "The tribe's trail must be lost already," called Charlie as Patrick, holding his pole lantern high, stood in the snow trying to determine their direction. The dog jumped and whimpered. He seemed to want Patrick to leave the vague trail. He barked and pulled on the youngster's hand. Finally, Charlie, in a puzzled voice, said, "I think he might know where they are. Follow him."

Patrick wanted to argue, but the dog was insistent. Charlie held the sledge at a stop while Patrick followed the dog into the night carrying the lantern pole across his shoulders. Soon Charlie heard a shout, "I got them," as he saw the swinging light. Patrick and the dog had found the small cluster of cold, hungry people clinging to the fallen body of a dead horse. In the following days everyone would remember how that sorry chicken dog was the one who had led the rescue.

Charlie turned the sledge in the direction of the glowing lantern near a copse of trees. Before getting too close, he fired a gun shot into the air. There was soon an answering shot. He got the sledge close and began to spread out the blankets on the bed while Patrick counted people and began to lead them to the ride. As they worked, Dell and the others arrived. They found three women, two men and five children. One woman was very pregnant. She was the woman they had met during the summer.

They were able to get the women and two children on the sledge. They knew that the cabin was only about a half mile away, but the horses were challenged to carry even that weight fighting the weather. There were still two men and three children. Patrick, Dell and Will each took a child while Running Elk shepherded the two men encouraging them to follow the sledge.

Finally, the sledge crested a small hill, and the welcoming glow of the cabin beckoned. Patrick pulled ahead with his young charge. Once at the house he called on the other boys and Molly to help get the Indians to the warmth and safety of the cabin. The other youngsters dressed quickly and followed him out to the caravan.

The additional hands were able to assist Running Elk with the very tired and hungry men as well as help with the other children. Pulling into the farmyard, Molly raced into the cabin with another child and announced, "I think that lady is birthing a baby. She keeps moaning."

Annabella and Willow raced out into the snow with Willow shouting in her language asking the woman to respond. After some chatter she turned to Annabella, "The baby is coming. We must get her inside first."

In her very capable way Annabella took charge of the coming events. Dell watched in amusement as his bride shouted directives getting everyone ready to birth a baby. Toby and the Preacher came to assist, assigned to quickly help the pregnant woman inside. Willow ran ahead to alert Morning Flower. While outside Annabella sent Patrick back to Running Elk to help with the Indian braves. Skeeter and Molly made certain that all the children were hustled into the cabin and then returned to help Will and Charlie assist the other two women.

Dell took charge of the sledge and went back to get the two braves who were having great difficulty walking even with Patrick's and Running Elk's assistance. The two braves were exhausted. It was obvious that the two men had worked hard to keep their family together. Dell could see the fatigue in their bodies as they gratefully tumbled onto the sledge.

Getting back to the cabin, Dell and the other men found a frenzy of activity. Manuel and Carmelita had taken over the kitchen and were preparing warm drinks and slices of bread for the visitors. Carmelita had cautioned that they looked as though they hadn't eaten in days and too much food would make them ill. Dell shivered at her knowledge. Had she been that hungry at some time in her past?

Now the cabin was very crowded. Dell counted his six children, Running Elk's two and the five who came in the blizzard - thirteen, plus the youngster who had arrived first to ask for help. And then he heard a cry coming from Morning Flower's bedroom. Fifteen children! And almost as many adults. Dell smiled to himself as he saw his wedding night melt away. He went to the kitchen to help Manuel pass the food that Carmelita had prepared.

Will and Patrick had gotten the braves settled before the fireplace and Toby was handing out drinks. Charlie asked for help bedding the sledge team. Molly and Skeeter rushed to assist. Those two kids were always ready to work with the animals.

Annabella came out of the birthing room and sat on the floor beside Dell. "Well, Mr. Rutherford, it's been a busy wedding day." He noticed that she and the girls had found time to change into their britches for the serious work of the evening.

"I think, Mrs. Rutherford, we'll be spending our wedding night sharing this crowded cabin with a few close friends."

She smiled at him and snuggled against his shoulder. "I never assisted in a birthing before. It was magical."

He slipped his arm around her and before he said another word she was asleep. He kissed the top of her head as he felt a jostle. Little Byron was curling up on Dell's other side with Missy close beside him. Dell scanned the room and saw the boys climbing up to sleep in their loft, Molly going with them. Charlie and Will and the preacher walked out the door headed for the privacy of the bunkhouse. All the visiting Indians were huddled together in front of the warmth of the fire.

What would the morning bring?

CHAPTER 27

Morning brought blue skies and sunshine. And about seventeen inches of snow. Dell awoke, stretched on the floor of the bedroom Henry had built for Annabella and the girls on the backside of the fireplace. His wife was in one bunk, Byron in another and Missy in the third. Some wedding night. But everyone was safe and still asleep.

Dell rolled up his blanket and slipped out into the big room. Running Elk was in a corner talking with the two braves. Dell nodded to the men and made his way through the kitchen where Carmelita and Willow were cooking breakfast and out toward the privy, grateful that someone had cleared a path to that essential convenience.

Returning to the cabin he found Annabella coming into the large room carrying the baby. She was smiling. "The new mother is exhausted. Morning Flower is making her rest this morning." Dell gave her and the baby a good morning kiss. She blushed and the baby yawned.

Running Elk signaled to Dell. It seemed that he and the braves had come to some conclusions. Dell squatted on the floor beside the men, nodding to Running Elk that he was ready to listen.

"They not return to tribe. Not like new chief." Dell nodded and waited for the rest of the information. "They want to be family here. They work. Women work."

Dell was quiet for some time as a sign to the Indians that he respected their opinions and would give their ideas thoughtful consideration. All three men sat on the floor exhibiting a patience that added to their demeanor of dignity and quiet reserve. Finally, Dell spoke. "Are these folks kin to you or Morning Flower?"

"All tribe brothers," replied Running Elk.

Dell supposed that was true. "You and Morning Flower can invite anyone to live here. I'll tell the government men you work for me. Is that what you want?"

"They stay."

"Running Elk, is this what you want? Are these good men? Will they work hard? Will the women work hard? And there are six more youngsters to feed who might not be helpful for a few years."

The Indian thought about Dell's statement. "They my brothers. They work."

The cabin was waking up around them. Soon Dell realized that he had to move his wife and children out today, snow or no snow. There was just not enough room for everyone.

Annabella came to him with the baby still in her arms. "What was the discussion?"

Dell shrugged. "Running Elk is willing to have all these folks stay here."

"Then we can move our children to our ranch as soon as they breakfast." She grinned. "I like to say our children and our ranch."

The rest of the day was very busy with routine chores, training the Indians on some of the daily work, packing the children and their belongings and making two hard trips on the sledge through the snow to Dell's ranch and back. By the end of the day, the Rutherford ranch house was filled with the new family. Will had managed to keep his own room and his privacy, even though Byron wanted to share the space.

Manuel and Carmelita moved into a small storage room at the side of the kitchen, asking if, in the future, they could claim a small, deserted cabin across the stream back in the trees. Dell agreed, saying, "That used to be a place some old trapper used during the winter. It may need a lot of work."

Carmelita had smiled at him. "To make my own home will not be too much work." Again Dell wondered how harsh had her life been before she arrived on the plateau.

xxx

"What-" Annabella gasped, surprised and tense as she found herself in Dell's arms.

"That, Mrs. Rutherford, was a kiss." He held her in his arms and studied her face. Over the last months he had learned every plain, every curve, and the subtle blush that appeared at unusual times. She was blushing now. And she looked frightened, but did she also look . . . curious? Dell hoped. Early in their courtship he had understood that Annabella was interested in a partnership, not a physical relationship. She had not said that intimacy was out of the question. She had only stated that she had experienced a marriage bed and found it lackluster. And as she had told him, concluded that she had no passion.

For his part Dell had found that he was too busy in recent years to do more than visit an older widow several times a year. She had been very clear that she had no interest in hitching up with a cowboy and living in isolation on the ranch. But she did admit to certain needs. It had been a pleasurable relationship, until she married a new banker in town. She always had a smile for Dell when they met, and he hadn't been interested in finding a replacement.

Until tonight. It was his delayed wedding night. The newlyweds were standing before the fireplace in the bedroom at Dell's ranch. This was the room his parents had shared for over thirty years. The wind was stirring outside, and the youngsters were all tucked into their new beds. He didn't know when he started to see Annabella as a wife worthy of bedding, but here he was and here she was and, by golly, he was interested.

"Would you like me to try it again?" he asked with a soft curve to his lips. She rubbed her lips and then ran her tongue over them. "Mrs. Rutherford, you are purely delightful to watch."

"Watch what?" She stayed clinging to his arms because she was so surprised. Yes, surprised was the word. Was that a normal kiss? She had no idea. He seemed to know these things. Try again? Had he asked if she wanted another kiss? She stared into his eyes and felt herself sway.

"I take that as a yes." He kissed her again with the same intensity as the first kiss. Then there was a third and a fourth. Each more fervent than the last. By the fifth kiss Annabella drew closer and kissed him back, shyly. He gripped her tightly to his chest and scattered kisses on her neck and ears and in her hair.

"Mr. Rutherford, you seem to be an expert at this kissing." She felt his laughter rumble through his chest.

"And you, Mrs. Rutherford, seem to be catching on to this kissing." He took her hands and held her at arms' length, then pulled her back into his arms. "May I bed you, Mrs. Rutherford?"

"That is a husband's privilege," she whispered, tensing.

"But I want you to be willing," he replied. "Are you?" He held his breath.

"Yes," she whispered.

xxx

Annabella stared at the dark ceiling. So that was bedding, she thought. How different than the exercise between her and Mr. Winters. In the short months that they had been married, their sexual exchanges were . . . Annabella thought about the experience. The only word that fit was tepid. Mr. Winters had been kind and reserved. He seemed to be fulfilled, a term she had read in the novels. But she had never found any stirring in herself to warrant the paragraphs of ecstasy related in those novels. She had thought she had no passion. Dell had found it in her.

She moved closer to this man who was now her husband. Was this sexual exchange a one-time event? Would those feelings happen again? Would she ever again feel that frenzy and ethereal, yet visceral, release?

Then she began to think about Mr. Winters, again. Had he tried to bring her to this edge, and she resisted? Had he wanted to join in a passion with her? Had she not understood him, or had she disrespected his efforts? Would they have had a different marriage if she had tried to meet him in his pleasure? Would she have been less lonely if she had opened her heart and her mind to being a part of his life, a part of his soul? Maybe he hadn't wanted or expected more than his own release. Maybe he didn't understand or didn't care that she could be raised to the level of ecstasy she had found this evening with Dell. Maybe Mr. Winters had just been a shy, quiet man who tried and never understood, but continued to try.

During her marriage she had stayed cloaked in her loneliness. And by doing so she had kept them both from finding a portion of contentment and happiness in the daily, boring chores required to operate a local mercantile. She wept onto Dell's shoulder - for her isolation and for Mr. Winters' loss - not realizing that she had curled into her husband's warmth in the comfortable bed that had belonged to his parents.

Dell awoke feeling the warm body snug against him. But he also felt something wet on his shoulder. He felt Annabella stir. "Are you crying? Did I hurt you?"

"I was so lonely," she whispered.

He turned and pulled her into his arms. "So was I," he said into her hair, that beautiful dark mass he had explored earlier. "But we're together now." And he wondered if it was normal, but he made love to her again. Twice in one night, God almighty, what would Will think?

CHAPTER 28

During the early weeks of a new marriage and new family Annabella found entertaining the children challenging. The snow piled up and life was restricted. Patrick and Toby worked the ranch, but Molly and Skeeter were too small to be useful in the deep snow. Checking on the chickens and working in the barn hadn't the glamour it did during a carefree summer.

"I can do what Toby can," said a belligerent Skeeter.

"I can't go out because I'm a girl," Molly complained to anyone who would listen. "That's not fair."

How had she kept a classroom of children engaged each day? At her wits end snowbound with children Annabella had an inspiration. She began a teaching session that she called Spring planning. She challenged Molly and Skeeter to comb through the mail order catalogue to prepare an order for items the house needed. She gave them examples such as interview Carmelita to find the kitchen utensils she needed to cook for a large family. They were also given the task of searching the ranch storage areas - outbuildings and attic - to determine what could be used by the new family.

Soon they had everyone involved in spring planning. Dell suggested that they plan for the new water closet and showed them the plumbing pages of the catalogue. Will suggested they look for a better lock for his bedroom door. Byron was relentless in wanting to share the space.

Missy thought she needed new toys and Byron agreed he did, too. Toby heard about the water closet and began working on a design. Patrick thought they should leave him alone because he had too much work to do but wouldn't mind a big tub for the water closet.

The water closet caught everyone's imagination, especially after having to dig a path through the snow to the privy daily, sometimes twice. Evenings were spent studying Toby's plans and then looking for parts. Annabella even found Molly and Skeeter in the potential water closet alcove, measuring and making notes for Toby to use as he refined his plan.

By early February the plan was ready. Toby presented his plan. Molly and Skeeter presented the catalogue order to build out the design. Dell was stunned. The kids had worked hard and presented a viable plan. It needed to be refined but it looked reasonable. He and Will studied the plan. They took it to Ake who had advanced construction skills. He studied it.

By the end of February, the plan was approved. Ake said that Mama wanted a water closet, too. So the parts order was doubled. And Will risked a March blizzard to get the order to the depot for the outgoing mail.

"Well, Mrs. Rutherford, you may be soaking in your own private bathtub soon," drawled Dell as he carried hot water into the bedroom for her late-night bath. Annabella smiled to herself. She had included in the catalogue order the request for several books that seemed to be dedicated to this new idea of inside water pipes. She hoped that the books would make certain she had a hot bath in her future.

xxx

Annabella sat staring at the morning. Dell had taken the ranch hands out early to check for calves and broken fences. From her seat at the window, she was able to see Henry's place. It sat on a knoll higher than Dell's ranch and closer to the mountains. It was close enough that the two families shared this frontier life. Annabella's school was teeming with scholars. In the morning the children came for lessons. After lunch the older boys returned to work, then returned in the evening with the men and women who came for night classes.

This had surprised both Dell and Annabella. Once she indicated that she was willing to teach adults, she had a dozen students, men and women, Indian, Mexican and white. Dell had insisted that classes only be held two nights a week. He was jealous of Annabella's time and had learned that after teaching all evening she had very little energy for his arms. She smiled at the thought. Dell had convinced her that a marriage bed was a magical place and she had been very willing to limit her teaching time.

And today she understood the reason. She was pregnant! She wanted to tell her husband, but he had gotten out so early this morning. Behind her she could hear the children finishing breakfast. Soon it would be time for classwork. But Dell would be back for lunch. She pulled her thoughts back to her classroom and would keep her students enthralled until lunch.

xxx

Will tiptoed into the kitchen as the children ate the breakfast Carmelita had placed on the table. "Today's Dell's birthday," he whispered, expecting giggles and smiles. Six sullen children looked at him. "What's wrong?"

Patrick cleared his throat, "We never had birthdays with Mam and Pap. We never had money."

"Nobody ever told me I had a birthday," said Skeeter, as he glanced wistfully at Byron. "Byron was just with us. No body celebrated."

"That ain't right," said Will in that way he had of hugging them with his voice. He snapped his fingers. "I tell you what. Dell's so old, he doesn't need another birthday, so today can be everyone's birthday."

Missy clapped her hands. "Do we each get a cake?"

"Cake," cheered Byron.

"We just need one big cake." Will put his finger to his lips. "Nobody say anything. And we'll all be surprised at dinner when we see our cake."

Six youngsters agreed. Will looked at Carmelita and she nodded that she understood. One cake for dinner.

xxx

"I don't know where he is," Grandy, the bunkhouse cook, told Dell. "He was here to saddle his horse then he disappeared. Maybe he went courting."

Dell gave a disgusted look toward the horizon. "I wanted him to take a crew to clear that big pine that fell in that last storm. I think we can get a lot of good wood out of it." One last angry look. "I'll do it myself."

It was going to be a long day. Simon at the Double X had a big saw. They would drag it to the Rocking R and spend the next few days making planks.

xxx

As the family assembled for dinner, Will rushed into the house. "Where have you been? I needed you all day." Dell was sweaty and tired.

"I had to go to town," said Will offering no other explanation. He looked around the kitchen and winked at the expectant faces.

"All sit," said Carmelita, "Food is ready."

Annabella came into the dining room, taking her place at the table. "Will, I haven't seen you all day. You missed lunch." Dell growled.

The kids were restless during the meal, trying to whisper, and each fidget annoyed Dell.

"I think I'll just get to bed early. I had a hard day." He slapped his napkin onto the table, getting ready to rise.

"No," chorused the kids.

"Why not?" Scowl.

The kids looked at Will. He gave his brother a sheepish grin. "This morning I told the kids it was your birthday. And I learned that no one among them has a birthday. So I gave yours away."

"He said you're too old," volunteered Missy. "Me and Byron needed your birthday. We're little."

In his fatigue Dell was trying to understand the conversation. Annabella was trying not to laugh. Carmelita cleared the table and placed a marvelous looking cake in the center.

"Wait," shouted Will as he left the room. They heard him clomping through the house. He returned to the dining room saying, "It's not a birthday without presents." He placed a sack on his chair and pulled out a gift. He checked the name and handed it to Toby. "Open your birthday gift." Toby slowly unwrapped the small package and found a new folding knife. Everyone "aahed."

With that Will slowly handed out a present to each child. Everyone waited for that present to be enjoyed before the next was handed out. Skeeter got a new leather belt. Molly got scented lotion, Missy got hair ribbons, Patrick got new work gloves, and Byron got a pair of red socks. Then he handed Carmelita a small package. "Thank you for making the cake." She opened her gift of scented soap. She cried.

"Now for Dell because he shared his birthday." Will handed his brother a package that contained a pair of red boot socks just like Byron's. Everyone cheered.

Then he turned to Annabella. "I couldn't forget you." He handed her a package. When she opened it, they all saw the newest edition of the mail order catalog. Will's birthday party was a success.

xxx

That evening as Dell soaked in Annabella's tub, she said, "I think you'll like our washroom when it's ready."

Dell was too sleepy to talk, but he managed, "This is a fine treat for my tired bones."

She moved closer to the tub and kissed his forehead. "I didn't know it was your birthday today. I could have planned something special."

"If I weren't so tired Mrs. Rutherford, we would do something special." He thought he was almost too tired to climb out of the tub.

"Maybe I can think of something special," she smirked, "that doesn't require you to do anything."

He sat up straight and sloshed water on the floor. "You have my attention."

She sat on her small bench in front of her small table and mirror, primping her hair. She looked coyly over her shoulder, clearly becoming an Annabella that she enjoyed. Dell was even more interested as she turned toward him with a grin. "Mr. Rutherford, for your birthday," she moved to kneel beside the tub, "I will be giving you something in about seven months." She waited for him to understand.

He smacked the water, splashing her, when he understood her meaning. "Our seventh child?"

"Or our first depending on how you look at it." She thought a moment. "I like the idea of our seventh child better. This one will just arrive a different way, not on a train."

They both laughed as he climbed from the tub and embraced his happily wet, pregnant wife.

CHAPTER 29

Annabella had told the children that before dinner they would have a family meeting. They all sat in the parlor, savoring the aroma of Carmelita's dinner, waiting for some announcement so they could attack the food.

Molly said, "I remember our first meeting. You told us you were getting married, and we thought you would send us away. But we're a family instead." The other children nodded and smiled in agreement.

"So what is happening now?" asked Skeeter. "Is Will getting married? Or Patrick?" Everyone laughed.

"We're planning an addition to our family," announced Dell.

"More Indians?" asked Toby.

Annabella said, "No, Dell and I are going to have a baby." She smiled at her children and to her surprise saw panic.

Missy sobbed. "You won't want us anymore. You'll have real children."

"You are our real children," said Dell as he embraced her. When Byron started to cry, Annabella caught him up in her arms. She looked to the older children for help, hoping their initial panic had faded.

Molly in her teen sophistication seemed to understand marriage and children best of everyone. Annabella was grateful she had talked with the youngster about womanly things. The young teen convinced Missy that she would no longer be the baby sister. That had a certain appeal to the youngest girl. Byron, not to be ignored decided that his baby status would also be void. Dell had to laugh at the logic that had calmed everyone.

After a great meal and Carmelita's cookies the children spent the rest of the evening talking about their new sibling. There was an argument over which would be best, a girl or a boy. And the discussion and debate about proposed names made Dell's head spin. But the news was out and everyone was ready for the arrival, disappointed that they had to wait so long.

xxx

"Why so pensive?" That was a word Dell had never used before, but Annabella's posture and frown demanded its use.

She turned and greeted him with a smile. They had shared the news of her pregnancy with the children. And had calmed them down. Dell always was caught up short when the children displayed their fears of abandonment and their insecurity regarding the family he and Annabella have built for them. It brought him pain to even think about their pasts. He and Will had been blessed with good parents, love and a steady, well-fed home life. He settled on the sofa next to his wife.

"I was thinking about Byron." She took his hand. They sat and studied the flames in the big stone fireplace. "I heard him speaking with Carmelita today - in Spanish. And when Lars stopped by the other day with Freja's bakery treats, he exchanged words in what I assume was Swedish."

"Pretty talented fellow," mused Dell. "Does that have you worried, teacher?"

She brought his hand to her face for a caress. "No, as I've told you before, I've seen immigrant children learn our language very quickly in the classroom. I've never experienced it in the other direction."

"Is it bad?"

"I don't know." She thought about the question some more. "He doesn't seem to be confused. He doesn't talk to you and me much. I don't understand why."

"Maybe because we know what he wants without him having to say much."

She pondered that idea. "An interesting thought," she said, "We anticipate his needs and aren't encouraging him to speak."

"You're making me sound more thoughtful than I am." He pulled her closer.

She had more to say. "He seems able to exchange ideas in each language and not speak the wrong language to the wrong person."

He brought her hand to his lips. Each day Dell marveled at the pleasures he received in marriage, especially these quiet moments. "Why are you concerned now?"

The pensive look returned. "Carmelita asked me if I objected to Byron learning Spanish. I told her to continue and to encourage the other children to learn also, if they were interested."

"Do you think you made a mistake?"

"Learning is never a mistake," said the teacher. "I am thinking about how to encourage all the children to learn languages without appearing to be encouraging them to learn." She puffed out a sigh. "That's a big educational challenge!"

Dell laughed. "Maybe we just let things be. And when he's a young man, Byron might know several languages." He laughed again, "And maybe he'll share them with us." It was a mystery to both of them that Byron, as loving as he was, remained quiet in large family gatherings and with his parents.

Annabella thought about his advice. "Maybe that's the solution," she proposed. "We won't seem to notice and Byron will learn and maybe the others will at least pick up enough of Swedish or Spanish -

"Or Indian."

Annabella gasped. "I hadn't thought of that. Willow's boys certainly share all sorts of native words with our children." She stood. "I think I'll wander into the kitchen and listen for new languages. I might even learn something."

Dell swatted at her backside because he could. She gave him a smile over her shoulder and went on her language quest. As she left he got back to his ranching concerns. He had spent all last evening and today working with calving in his herd. He needed someone who spoke 'cow.' Smiling he realized that he did have someone. Molly had a great sense of animal need. Maybe he should invite her to join him this evening to improve her animal language skills.

xxx

Dell and Molly stumbled into the kitchen just as Carmelita was stoking the fire to begin preparing breakfast. The youngster was exhausted, Dell was sort of carrying her. He settled her at the table and asked Carmelita to give her tea and toast. "She's got to get some sleep, but I know she needs a little food."

The woman uttered something in Spanish that sounded like an insult to Dell. He was certain it was an insult once he noticed her flashing eyes. She gave Molly a hug and spoke softly in words that sounded like a caress. Dell suspected the cook would ignore him while she tended the youngster. He got his own coffee.

Annabella breezed into the kitchen, smiling, happy to be over those weeks of morning sickness. She stopped. "You had her out all night?" More flashing eyes.

"We had three babies," grinned Molly. "They were so cute." She tried to get the cup of warm tea to her lips, but it was a challenge. Carmelita helped her. Both women scowled at Dell.

"She was a big help." He talked fast, defending himself. "She calmed the first-time mamas and didn't get upset at all the . . . er . . . mess."

"I put my hand . . . er . . . in the baby path."

"Baby path?"

"Will said it was the path the baby calf would slide out."

"You put your hand in?" Annabella turned green.

Will walked into the kitchen. "Mornin' little nurse." He squeezed Molly's shoulder.

"She reached in the cow?" Annabella tried not to screech.

"She was great. My hand was too big." He waved his arm to show its size. "Our girl here went right in and turned that little fellow."

"I named him Pokey," yawned Molly. Annabella raced out of the kitchen and they could hear her retching into the shrubbery.

So much for no more morning sickness, thought Dell.

XXX

Dell had walked on eggshells all day. Annabella and Carmelita were royally pissed, an assessment Will made before his hightailed it out to the range, away from glowering women. Dell wondered if Annabella would share a quiet evening with him as she usually did. Or would she still be angry. He tiptoed into the parlor and found her reading by one of the oil lamps. "Are you still mad?"

She placed a marker on the page, closed the book and looked up at him. "I don't know what to think, Dell. Birthing cows and reaching inside is so unladylike, but so natural on a cattle ranch. I haven't come to terms with it yet."

He sat beside her and took her hand. "We want our children to explore their talents and interests. Just last week we talked about Byron and his languages. Maybe Molly's talent is animals. Even though she's a tiny girl, she has a special skill with livestock." He kissed her hand. "You should have seen her. Nothing phased her."

"Please restrain yourself. I don't want to lose my dinner." She gently patted her stomach.

"I'm just saying she has a talent. Maybe we should order some books for her to learn more."

"But she's a girl, Dell. We both know that she would not be allowed to move in animal husbandry arenas. No one would listen to her advice."

"Now, Annabella," Dell soothed her. "Times are changing. We can help her learn here. Even if she stays on the plateau, she'll be useful. If she's good, all the ranchers here will want her services. They'll all know her. We won't have to worry about what they would say in Laramie or Cheyenne."

Annabella wiped a tear from her eye. "Do you realize how restricting this could be to her? She wouldn't be able to leave the plateau because no place would welcome her. No school would let her expand her skills." She stared into the fire. "But," here it comes thought Dell, "she should be able to follow her interests. We'll stand by her. Won't we, Dell?"

He hugged her. "I think you just talked around a circle. Our Molly is thirteen. She's got time to prepare for her future. The world has got time to prepare for her. Let's just buy her some books and let her explore."

Annabella wiped her eyes and nestled into Dell's arms as they prepared for their evening of studying the fire and enjoying the sounds of their family.

xxx

Will ambled into the parlor. He envied Dell these quiet nights with his wife. "I forgot," he confessed to Annabella, "I got some mail for you today. Grandy brought it back from town." As he watched her take the letter he thought it might be time he spoke to Astrid about his intentions. Dell and Annabella made a loving argument for marriage.

"For me?" She took the envelope from his hand, curious. During her time on the plateau, she had never received a letter. Of course, she had only written to her brother. She turned it over in her hand and read the return postmark. "It's from an attorney in Cincinnati." She paled. Her hands shook. "Bad news." She was certain as she said it.

Both Dell and Will were now at her side, just as wary and curious. "Maybe you have an inheritance?" offered Will. "Or a rich relative is looking for you? Or someone finally solved a murder and decided you did it?" Dell smacked him on the back of his head.

In the magic that Annabella couldn't explain, the children had quietly gathered in the parlor as though a mysterious signal had alerted them to something interesting afoot. "Maybe you're a princess," suggested Missy as she settled on a stool waiting for the drama to unfold.

"Or somebody heard about your school and wants you to come to their town and teach," guessed Patrick.

Dell did a three-sixty scowl, and everyone sat in silence, Byron settling on Will's lap just in case things turned ugly and he needed a big hug.

While everyone was finding a place to sit, Annabella had opened her letter. She gasped. "My brother is dead." She read silently as she chewed her lip. "So is his wife." More reading. "Children?" she cried. Everyone got on their feet. Byron clinging to Will's neck.

Dell took the letter as Annabella sat, wiping tears from her eyes. He cleared his throat as he scanned the document. "This attorney says he was happy to receive your letter." He turned to his wife. "I guess he means that letter you sent just before we married." He turned back to the letter. "Your brother's wife had died three years ago in childbirth. Then last summer," he stopped, "Just when you moved here." He turned back to the letter. "Your brother died in a fire." Everyone gasped. Dell read on, "It was his house. He rescued the children and ran back in for something and the dwelling collapsed." Annabella sobbed. Molly and Missy ran to her side to comfort her.

"So what about these children?" asked Will, Byron still clinging to his neck.

Dell scanned the lengthy missive. "It seems this here attorney has been tending to the children since their father's death. He says now that he knows that Annabella is alive and well, he is dispatching the children to Wyoming. He thinks the children should get here a week after the letter."

"What?" Everyone cried as one curious family.

Dell looked over his family. "Two small children, a boy eight and a girl five."

"He put them on a train? Is someone accompanying them?" This had Annabella's attention. All the children could remember that day on the train traveling without adults, trying to stay together.

"He doesn't say," replied Dell as he studied the letter. "It seems the children have some inheritance, but he had to use some of their resources to cover their living expenses since your brother's death. He also says that you have been named as guardian to the children by state law as the last known relative." Dell looked up from the letter. "He's sounds mighty pompous. He uses a lot of words to say the youngsters are yours. Don't return them. And when you respond to this letter, he will transfer their funds as you direct."

"Did he send them alone on the train?"

Dell shrugged. "He doesn't say." He studied the dates on the letter and concluded. "They might be here any day."

"We have to go into town tomorrow." Now Annabella was in a panic. "They can't be alone."

"I want to go, too," cried Missy. The boys all nodded.

Will was more pragmatic. "Where are we going to put two more?" Maybe it was time to move on and start his own household. He would visit Astrid for Sunday dinner.

CHAPTER 30

"Remember the train comes in the afternoon," Dell reminded everyone as their mounts tiptoed down the trail. They were on their way into town. After a lot of discussion and begging from those left behind, Dell, Annabella, Molly and Toby were on the long trail into town on horseback. The steep trail was still too wintry for passage.

When they arrived in town, Annabella insisted on going directly to the depot. She hurried inside with Molly close behind. Dell and Toby walked in as the station master was explaining, "Miss Annabella, we haven't seen any children come through. Now, the train is due within the hour if they got the snow off the tracks."

She was so agitated that Dell spoke up. "Hiram, we're waiting for Annabella's niece and nephew. She's just concerned that we meet them, and they don't feel alone."

Hiram nodded. "I can understand that." He turned to her. "We know what a fine lady you are, ma'am, taking all those youngsters and making old Henry so happy with his family."

Dell was relieved. It was just the right thing to say. Annabella calmed and thanked him for his kind words. And they heard the train whistle. "If they're not on this train," he advised her, "we'll make arrangements for the minister to meet them. Will or Patrick can come down to town every day or so until we can claim them." She ignored him as she focused on the big engine steaming alongside the platform. Steps dropped from the cars and folks began to disembark.

"There they are," screeched Molly as she ran toward two small children.

When she got closer a large, suspicious conductor placed a hand on each youngster's shoulder. "Do you know this lady?" he asked the children. They shook their heads, flustered and frightened. He said to Molly and to Annabella who had come to her side. "I have to turn these here youngsters over to the station man. He will deliver them."

Hiram appeared at the conductor's side. "That's me." The conductor handed him a letter. "You sign this. Somebody paid a fee for this delivery. I gotta show you got them."

Hiram read the letter, signed it and turned to Annabella. "Miss Annabella, I want you to meet Randolph and Hannah Chase." Two somber children looked at the woman who had gasped and stared at them.

"She looks like you," said Dell as he joined the group.

"They look like me and my brother when we were children." She had tears in her eyes. "They're my only blood family I have left." The children stood stiffly, not certain who this woman was.

By this time the conductor had left the drama, disinterested, while Hiram stood close by wanting to capture every minute for retelling around town. Molly had already taken the little girl's hand and was whispering to her. The little boy was listening to the conversation, shooting interested glances back at Dell and Annabella.

"They only had these two bags," said Toby as he joined the group. "That's not enough to keep warm."

That statement made Annabella stop and study her new charges. Toby was correct. They were not dressed to travel on horseback up to the plateau. "I guess we stop at the mercantile before we head home," sighed Dell. "It'll be cold on the horses."

"Horses?" The little boy was wide-eyed. They had his attention.

"We came on horses," explained Toby, "'cause the wagon trail has too much snow." The little girl began to cry. "I can't ride a horse."

Annabella scooped her up and kissed her. "Don't worry, sweetie. You can ride with me or Molly." She stopped. "You don't know who we are, do you?" She didn't wait for an answer. "I'm your Aunt Annabella. I was your father's sister. And this is my husband, your Uncle Dell. And this is Molly and Toby, our children, your cousins."

Molly grinned. "I've never been a cousin." Little Hannah took her hand.

Dell watched the interaction and thought things would work out. "Come on, we have to shop and get back up the mountain."

xxx

Returning to the ranch caused a small riot. The other children were waiting to meet the new members of the family. Trying to keep things calm, Dell went into ranch manager mode. "Patrick and Skeeter, you boys take care of these horses. Toby you carry the packages into the house." Missy already had Hannah by the hand urging her onto the porch. Will came out to greet everyone and help the boys put up the horses. Manuel and Carmelita waved from the porch as she shouted, "Dinner in half hour." Manuel rushed toward the barn to help with the horses. Everyone wanted to be at dinner.

"Did you wait for us?" asked Annabella. "You didn't feed the children?"

"No one wanted to eat without the new ones," explained Carmelita, smiling at the two small children.

When they finally all gathered in the dining room, Annabella said, "Let me introduce everyone. This is Hannah and Randolph." The other kids grinned. "And these are our children, Patrick, Toby, Molly, Skeeter, Missy and Byron." Each child waved or nodded as his name was called. Annabella turned to the adults. "You know Uncle Dell, and this is his brother, Uncle Will. And this is Carmelita, our cook, and Manuel, our ranch wrangler. We are all happy to have you here." She smiled.

Randolph looked around. "Is this an orphanage? They told us we might go to one."

"This is your family," said Annabella. "No one is to think about an orphanage. Your daddy wanted me to take care of you."

"But he's dead," cried Hannah. "We're orphans. That's what the man said."

Molly put an arm around her. "We used to be orphans, but Miss Annabella took us from the train. Just like you."

"We're all orphans," concluded Skeeter, with a joyous grin.

Hannah cried harder. Annabella took the little girl in her arms. Dell shook his head. He stepped into the confusion. "Let's all be seated for dinner." And he gave everyone the stare that was becoming his trademark. Even Will flopped into a chair. Carmelita had already made space for two extra plates. She and Manuel brought out the food. Things got quiet as the hungry family began to fill their plates. The two new children were seated down the table on either side of Annabella.

Dell cleared his throat. "Randolph and Hannah" he addressed the youngsters, "Your Aunt Annabella met all of our children on a train. She took them to her ranch." At each statement one of the kids opened a mouth to refute or explain more fully. Dell stared. Mouths closed. "The children were orphans. They all went to live with Annabella's father-in-law because she had been widowed."

"Like my daddy," offered Randolph.

"Exactly." Dell continued. "Annabella and I married at Christmas and she and all the children came to my ranch so we could be a family. And now you are with us and will be part of our family, too."

Before Randolph could answer Missy had to add, "And Dell brought Will. He's not one of the orphans."

And Skeeter threw out, "And the Indians live at our old ranch."

"Indians?" was Randolph's question. Hannah stared wide-eyed.

"They're our friends," added Toby. "Once you learn to ride, we'll go visit."

"Ride?" Hannah looked like she would cry again.

"Horsey," smiled Byron.

"Does he ride?" asked Randolph.

"Not alone," said Patrick. "He's still too small. But Missy rides and she's your size." Missy nodded. "It's easy. And Carmelita makes us cookies and Freja makes us cookies and Morning Flower makes us cheese."

"Do they all live here?"

"No," explained Skeeter, "they all live on their own ranches. We're all friends."

Dinner ended as the children all began to yawn.

xxx

"We got them all into bed," sighed Annabella. "But Will was correct. We may need more room once they all get bigger." They were getting ready for bed after a tiring day finding and welcoming the new arrivals.

"We'll face that problem when the time comes, Mrs. Rutherford." He caressed her abdomen. "I guess we'll have to think about our nursery, too." He kissed her. "I get much pleasure thinking about our child."

She felt her heart blossom. This was marriage. Was this love? "We shall get pleasure and joy from all of our children. All nine of them." He blew out his breath. She giggled. "Mr. Rutherford, nine is a large number and sometimes you give me so much pleasure that I wonder if that number might go to ten in the future or eleven."

He pulled her to him. "We shall love them all, Mrs. Rutherford."

CHAPTER 31

Notice from the catalog company announced that the order had been received with proper payment and the items would be delivered during April.

One day Will returned from a buying trip to town with a wagon piled high with crates and packages. Everyone at the Rocking R became delirious with delight. Patrick raced to the Double B to invite Ake and his family to the unwrapping and uncrating.

While the family waited for the Swedes, Annabella searched through the packages and found the books she had ordered. Scanning quickly through the pages of diagrams and unfamiliar words, she hoped she had not been mistaken.

"What are those?" asked Toby who could hardly sit still waiting for the Swede partners to arrive.

"I ordered some books that were advertised as helpful with installing inside pipes and water closets."

Toby flipped through the first book and was soon lost in diagrams and jargon, muttering things like, "so that's how," and "this will be easy."

Annabella shuddered.

xxx

Once the plumbing supplies arrived from the catalog company, it was time to begin the project. After much discussion and a lot of remeasuring and sketching, Toby suggested that they add a small addition off the back of the kitchen. He argued that they could take advantage of the of the water piping through the kitchen pump. And, he argued, that would make getting warm water from the kitchen stove to the tub easier and quicker. He didn't want to even think about how to heat the room. But he didn't say that. In his opinion the adults had to come up with some ideas.

"Let me sleep on it," said Dell. It was late and the youngster had used diagrams and references to the books that Annabella had ordered to help their installation.

Once settled in their room, Dell said, "That boy has a lot of ideas." He shrugged out of his shirt. "He thinks too fast for me." Off came his trousers. "What do you think?" He looked over at Annabella who was combing out her hair as she sat demurely on a small bench she called a boudoir settee. Water closets, settees, what was his world coming to?

"I think that youngster is much smarter than all of us." Dell knew that was the teacher speaking. He raised an eyebrow and waited. She put aside the hairbrush. "He can see ideas in mathematics, and he can remember facts. I have worked with very smart children in the past. It was difficult to keep them from becoming bored. I think we should be considering his future education."

Dell plopped on the bed. "All our children are bright." Annabella smiled at the stalwart father, loving and seeing the best in all his children.

"They all have intelligence in different areas," she said. "Patrick should go off to study with your uncle's friend in St. Louis next winter."

"To study what?" challenged Dell. "He wants to ranch."

"I know, but you spent two winters learning law and other skills to help you manage the ranch." He had to agree because it was true. "And Skeeter needs more training. I think he will be a writer or reporter. Maybe he can read law for a time while he figures things out."

"What about our girls? Are you going to make them get more schooling because you did?"

Annabella wasn't sure if that was a dare or just a question. "I want them to choose if they want more learning." Molly was already making a name for herself on the plateau with her animal skills. "I don't want anyone to tell our daughters that they are girls and should restrict their dreams to being a wife and mother." She sat very straight on the settee. Dell heard that line drawn in the sand.

He nodded. "They can study as hard as their brothers." Annabella let out her breath. He smiled and pulled her to her feet. "Our children have a mother who will fight for them." He kissed her on the tip of her nose. "We will let them know that they can take any opportunity and dream as big as they like. Because their mama says so." She smiled. This marriage thing is a pretty good deal, he thought.

xxx

The next morning Dell and Will rode out to check something, but really went out to have a private talk about Toby's proposal. "Annabella says he's smarter than all of us." Dell opened the discussion.

"He is that," replied Will after he checked to make certain none of the children were close by. "I think he has a good idea. I never even gave a thought to shit and where it would go." Will slapped his thigh startling his horse. "And he doesn't call it shit, he calls it something else."

"I think he learned all those words from the books Annabella bought."

"And he talks about freezing pipes," moaned Will. "We only worried about freezing our asses in the privy. No one thought about pipes." He was certain that modern and improvement were not compatible terms.

Dell turned his horse. "Let's go talk with Ake. This has just become a bigger job than we thought."

"Those catalog people sure know how to sell something and just hypnotize you into forgetting practical things."

"I think you just figured out why they are so successful."

Will groaned in agreement as he followed Dell to Ake's.

"That be one smart boy," said Ake as he looked over Toby's sketches. "We can do it. Maybe you want a sauna, too."

"Damn it, Ake," growled Dell, "one new contraption at a time. You build a sauna and we'll all come use yours."

Ake slapped Dell on the back. "You use once. You want me to build for you, too."

"Just help me get this plumbing and construction done. I don't want my pregnant wife falling on her way to the privy."

Ake whistled through his teeth. "We hurry. Miss Annabella good person."

"Thank you," said Dell.

xxx

"Carmelita," Annabella smiled, "You are a treasure, a gift to my family." Annabella sat in a chair and massaged her lower back. Who knew pregnancy could make you so happy and so stiff? "I'm happy you came to us."

"I am most happy, too." The woman continued her baking. "The children like cookies."

Annabella smiled. "We all like cookies. Have Patrick take some to Morning Flower."

"You take care of family."

"I think we have all become family on the plateau." Annabella was silent as she watched the woman work. She made a cup of tea with the hot water always in the stove reservoir. "I didn't have a family until I came here. My brother sent me away when our parents died, and he wanted to marry. I had no family until Henry and Morning Flower took me in."

"Manuel has told me the story of you and the children. He say you brought life to the old rancher."

"We did enjoy our life with Henry. I guess we all need folks who care for us."

Carmelita brushed a tear from her eye. "Manuel save me. He find me in dark room. Men come and go. I was used. I tied to bed." Annabella gasped and started to cry. Carmelita dropped to her knees and grasped Annabella's hand. "Manuel came one day and see me. He know me from our old village. He buy me from the men and take me to the mission. I very weak. The nuns they clean me and feed me. They teach me to

175

cook. I work for them. Each snow time Manuel come to stay with me. When he learn that you marry he come and take me with him."

Annabella knelt on the floor beside her and hugged her, both women sobbing. "You are safe with us."

"I know. Manuel tell me the same. This house make me very happy. You and the children make me very happy."

That evening in bed, Annabella sobbed into Dell's arms as she related Carmelita's story. "How can people be so cruel?"

"It's who we are," he said as he rubbed her back. "Just think, though, how many people you have helped to grow a better life." She nodded as he named each of the children, all the Indians, the Swedes, and now Carmelita. Soon she was asleep in his arms and he thought that she had saved him the most.

CHAPTER 32

Over the early weeks of their arrival Annabella watched for signs of distress in her brother's children. To her surprise they seemed to blend into the family with only a few bumps. She was amused when they showed confusion and distain for the privy. They had been used to indoor plumbing in modern Cincinnati. She assured them that a water closet was in their future.

Little Hannah liked having older sisters. For their part Molly and Missy enjoyed tending to her and sharing their sisterly secrets. Annabella understood belonging. Hannah knew she belonged.

The surprise was Randolph who had quickly been dubbed Dolf by the other boys. It seemed Byron couldn't say Randolph. Dolf and Byron soon became best pals. Just a few years younger than Skeeter, Dolf could easily relate to the youngest boy. For his part Byron liked to have someone to mentor teaching the excitement of ranch life. The biggest surprise was the information Byron seemed to share with Dolf. No one heard Byron talk much, except her nephew. He was always heard to report, "Byron said," or "Byron told me." She wondered when the rest of the family would hear Byron's wisdom.

One day Dolf approached Annabella. "Byron said a man came on a horse one day and brought him a puppy." She glanced at the half-grown mannerless animal sprawled at her feet that had won her heart as easily as any of the children. "Do you think the man will come back with another puppy?"

Before she could answer, as usual in her household, other children materialized. Hannah and Missy stood before her holding hands. "We want a kitten," declared Missy.

Annabella tried not to laugh. She looked out the windows at the vast acreage of their ranch. She was certain there was room to accommodate more livestock. But she also knew that any pet would find its way into the house. Was the house big enough for nine children, two dogs and probably two kittens? She smiled at them all. "Why don't we ask Uncle Will to check with the other ranchers to see if they have new pets for us?" Everyone left the room happy. Of course, she would have to prepare Dell for more mouths to feed.

xxx

When the snow melt happened, Annabella felt as though she were seeing her new home for the first time. Dell's mother had tended flowerbeds that had fallen to neglect. She and Molly and Missy enjoyed working to revive them each morning. And Byron couldn't resist collecting bouquets each afternoon for her pleasure.

Will had made his intentions known to Astrid. He still lived at the ranch but was spending more time building a home for his bride.

All was not settled, though. There was discord among the Indians living on Henry's ranch. One of the women, Song Bird, turned out to be Morning Flower's sister. She had moved into the bunkhouse with Charlie, and they had taken in her three grandchildren who had been left orphans.

But the other two women and the two braves found that they didn't like ranch work. They seemed to be unhappy with many things. Annabella suspected that Running Elk expected them to work harder than they wanted.

Morning Flower tried to explain the situation. "They go to Canada, say government help them."

"Canada?"

Morning Flower had nodded. "They want old ways. I think they not like clean stalls and horse shit."

Annabella had laughed. "That's ranch work." Morning Flower had laughed, too.

Family life at Henry's ranch settled down with Morning Flower and two worker families - Running Elk and his family and Charlie with Birdie and her grandchildren. Manuel and the Swedes helped out when needed.

"Dell," posed Annabella, "are you surprised the Indians left?"

"No," he said, "they weren't treated well in town and they thought Running Elk demanded too much. They went looking for a place that would treat them fair. And Running Elk was younger and they didn't like that he was their boss."

"I don't think I understand." She would have given it more thought, but she liked snuggling in bed with Dell more than she liked talking about the neighbors.

xxx

Annabella sat on the porch of the family home she shared with Dell. She remembered a woman remarking on one of her visits to town after settling in with Henry. The woman asked, "How can you survive in that isolation on the plateau?" Annabella laughed to herself. Since her arrival with six children, she had met and befriended Indians, the Rutherfords, other ranch families, several cowhands of all backgrounds. She ran a school for children and adults, managed a home for eight children and a coming baby, had a fine brother in Will, uncles in Charlie and Manuel, along with an adopted mother in Morning Flower.

In addition, today her family now included the Swedes. Will and Astrid were celebrating their wedding. Over the last months Ake and his sons had repaired and renovated the old Double B ranch house for the family. Once Will made known his interest in Astrid, they very quickly planned and began construction on a home for the young couple. It was as Dell had envisioned - a place to grow a family on a small rise on the west edge of the ranch yard - far enough away for privacy but close enough for family life.

Even the two quiet Swede brothers had hinted that they might like to find wives. Will had recently reported that the surprise death of Orville at the Bar Eight had his wife and son thinking of selling. As Will relayed to everyone, "She says she's done with Wyoming winters and wants to go to California."

Once he and Dell expressed a willingness to help Lars and Gunner purchase their own ranch, the transaction closed quickly. And that's how life moved on the isolated plateau.

Being sent off by her brother all those years ago was now a blessing to Annabella. She silently thanked him for the life he had allowed her to find. She was startled out of her reverie as Dell said, "Mrs. Rutherford, you're daydreaming again."

"I am, Mr. Rutherford." She patted her bugling belly. "I'm thinking about the future we will give to this little one." They watched as Gunner ran by with little Byron on his shoulders while Lars jousted at him with one of Running Elk's sons atop his shoulders - the Swede blond and youngster's dark coloring were an eye-catching contrast - and Missy raced hand in hand with Hannah as they were chased by one of Simon's boys from the Double X. Charlie and his squaw, Song Bird - whom he called Birdie - talked with Freja while Manuel and his lady monitored the meat cooking over the fire. Several ranch women placed food along a trestle table while Ake talked with the other ranchers.

Dell took her hand. "This is sure a different place since you and your youngsters arrived." He kissed her wrist and massaged her fingers.

She laughed. "How can you say that? All these people were here when we arrived."

"But we didn't live as neighbors. I think you helped us, with your school and your ready acceptance of everyone. First the kids and then Morning Flower's folks and me."

She stood and walked into his arms. They laughed as her stomach intruded on their hug. "I was so lonely when I arrived. And I saw that loneliness in so many here. I wasn't magic. We all wanted more than the life we were living. We all wanted love and laughter and family."

Missy raced onto the porch, giggled and hid behind Dell's legs. "Mrs. Rutherford, we do have family." He kissed her ear and whispered, "And we do have love."

Next Title in the Annabella Series:

Book 2 "A Growing Business"

Five years ago Annabella Chase Winters came to Deep Wells, Wyoming. Five years later she is married to a prosperous rancher, the mother of nine children, waiting to meet the young woman her oldest son, Patrick plans to marry. A natural disaster and a terminated engagement begin a year of her older children trying to define their roles in the world. As the youngsters find their way, Dell, Annabella's husband, begins to organize his land and related businesses into a functioning operation that will serve his family into the next generation, much like the corporations beginning to function throughout the country.

About The Author

RENEE KUMOR was a stay-at-home mom for several years developing a personal ethic of community service. She began writing a political opinion column for the local newspaper, but retired from writing when she announced her candidacy for local political office. After eight years as a county commissioner, she returned to non-profit service and began writing a monthly column for the newspaper on non-profit management and service issues. The setting for the *River Bend Chronicles* series reflects her early life in Ohio and her later years in western North Carolina.

For sales, editorial information, subsidiary rights information
or a catalog, please write or phone or e-mail

AbsolutelyAmazingEbooks
Manhanset House
Shelter Island Hts., New York 11965, US
Tel: 212-427-7139
www.AbsolutelyAmazingEbooks.com
bricktower@aol.com
www.IngramContent.com